Octopussy

Ian Fleming was born in 1908 and educated at Eton, where he was Victor Ludorum two years in succession – a distinction only once equalled. After Sandhurst, and Munich and Geneva Universities, he joined Reuters, making his first mark as a journalist during the famous 1933 Moscow trial of British engineers. He began to understand espionage methods. After a short spell as a partner in a stockbroking firm, he joined the staff of *The Times* and returned to Moscow. During the war he served with the rank of Commander in the Naval Intelligence Division and in 1945 he joined the Kemsley Newspapers as foreign manager. In Jamaica he built his house, 'Goldeneye', in which to spend his annual leave and it was here that James Bond was 'conceived'.

Casino Royale was completed on the eve of his marriage to Anne Rothermere in 1952, and this was the turning point in his life. In all he published fourteen books about the character who became the most famous secret agent ever, and so far eight James Bond adventures have been filmed. Twenty-six million copies of his books have been sold by Pan alone. During the 1950s Ian Fleming's health began to fail and he died in 1964 at the age of fifty-six.

Also by Ian Fleming in Pan Books

Ian Fleming

Octopussy

Pan Books
London and Sydney

Octopussy and *The Living Daylights* first published 1966 by
Jonathan Cape Ltd
First published in this form 1967 by Pan Books Ltd,
Cavaye Place, London SW10 9PG
9th printing 1976
Octopussy © the Literary Executors of Ian Fleming, 1965, 1966
The Property of a Lady © Ian Fleming 1963
The Living Daylights © Ian Fleming 1962
ISBN 0 330 02081 1
Printed in Great Britain by
Cox & Wyman Ltd, London, Reading and Fakenham

Octopussy

'YOU KNOW WHAT?' said Major Dexter Smythe to the octopus. 'You're going to have a real treat today if I can manage it.'

He had spoken aloud and his breath had steamed up the glass of his Pirelli mask. He put his feet down to the sand beside the nigger-head and stood up. The water reached to his armpits. He took off the mask and spat into it, rubbed the spit round the glass, rinsed it clean and pulled the rubber band of the mask back over his head. He bent down again.

The eye in the mottled brown sack was still watching him carefully from the hole in the coral, but now the tip of a single small tentacle wavered hesitatingly an inch or two out of the shadows and quested vaguely with its pink suckers uppermost. Dexter Smythe smiled with satisfaction. Given time, perhaps one more month on top of the two during which he had been chumming up with the octopus, and he would have tamed the darling. But he wasn't going to have that month. Should he take a chance today and reach down and offer his hand, instead of the expected lump of raw meat on the end of his spear, to the tentacle – shake it by the hand, so to speak? No, Pussy, he thought. I can't quite trust you yet. Almost certainly other tentacles would whip out of the hole and up his arm. He only needed to be dragged down less than two feet, the cork valve on his mask would automatically close and he would be suffocated inside it or, if he tore it off, drowned. He might get in a quick lucky jab with his spear, but it would take more than that to kill Pussy. No. Perhaps later in the day. It would be rather like playing Russian roulette, and at about the same five-to-one-odds. It might be a quick, a whimsical way out of his troubles! But not now. It would leave the interesting question unsolved. And he had promised that nice Professor Bengry at the Institute. Dexter Smythe swam leisurely off towards the reef, his eyes questing for one shape only, the squat sinister wedge of a scorpion fish, or, as Bengry would put it, *Scorpaena Plumieri*.

Major Dexter Smythe, OBE, Royal Marines (Retd), was the remains of a once brave and resourceful officer and of a handsome man who had made easy sexual conquests all his military life and particularly among the Wrens and Wracs and ATS who manned the communications and secretariat of the very special task force to which he had been attached at the end of his service career. Now he was fifty-four, slightly bald and his belly sagged in the Jantzen trunks. And he had had two coronary thromboses. His doctor, Jimmy Greaves (who had been one of their high poker game at Queen's Club when Dexter Smythe had first come to Jamaica), had half-jocularly described the later one, only a month before, as 'the second warning'. But, in his well-chosen clothes, his varicose veins out of sight and his stomach flattened by a discreet support belt behind an immaculate cummerbund, he was still a fine figure of a man at a cocktail party or dinner on the North Shore, and it was a mystery to his friends and neighbours why, in defiance of the two ounces of whisky and ten cigarettes a day to which his doctor had rationed him, he persisted in smoking like a chimney and going to bed drunk, if amiably drunk, every night.

The truth of the matter was that Dexter Smythe had arrived at the frontier of the death-wish. The origins of this state of mind were many and not all that complex. He was irretrievably tied to Jamaica, and tropical sloth had gradually riddled him so that while outwardly he appeared a piece of fairly solid hardwood, under the varnished surface the termites of sloth, self-indulgence, guilt over an ancient sin and general disgust with himself had eroded his once hard core into dust. Since the death of Mary two years before, he had loved no one. He wasn't even sure that he had really loved her, but he knew that, every hour of the day, he missed her love of him and her gay, untidy, chiding and often irritating presence, and though he ate their canapés and drank their martinis, he had nothing but contempt for the international riff-raff with whom he consorted on the North Shore. He could perhaps have made friends with the soldier elements, the gentleman-farmers inland, or the plantation owners on the coast, the professional men and the politicians, but that would mean regaining some serious purpose in life which his sloth, his spiritual accidie, prevented, and cutting down on the bottle, which he was definitely unwilling to do. So Major Smythe was bored, bored to death, and, but for one factor in his life, he would long ago have swallowed the bottle of barbiturates he had easily acquired from a local doctor. The lifeline that kept him clinging to the edge of the cliff was a tenuous one. Heavy drinkers veer towards an exaggeration of their basic temperaments, the classic four – Sanguine, Phlegmatic, Choleric and Melancholic. The Sanguine drunk goes gay to the point of hysteria and idiocy. The Phlegmatic sinks into a morass of sullen gloom. The Choleric is the fighting drunk of the cartoonists who spends much of his life in prison for smashing people and things, and the Melancholic succumbs to self-pity, mawkishness and tears. Major Smythe was a Melancholic who had slid into a drooling fantasy woven around the birds and insects and fish that inhabited the five acres of Wavelets (the name he had given his small villa is symptomatic), its beach and the coral reef beyond. The fish were his particular favourites. He referred to them as 'people' and, since reef fish stick to their territories as closely as do most small birds, after two years he knew them all intimately, 'loved' them and believed that they loved him in return.

They certainly knew him, as the denizens of zoos know their keepers, because he was a daily and a regular provider, scraping off algae and stirring up the sand and rocks for the bottom-feeders, breaking up sea eggs and urchins for the small carnivores and bringing out scraps of offal for the larger ones, and now, as he swam slowly and heavily up and down the reef and through the channels that led out to deep water, his 'people' swarmed around him fearlessly and expectantly, darting at the tip of the three-pronged spear they knew only as a prodigal spoon, flirting right up to the glass of the Pirelli and even, in the case of the fearless, pugnacious demoiselles, nipping softly at his feet and legs.

Part of Major Smythe's mind took in all these brilliantly coloured little 'people', but today he had a job to do and while he greeted them in unspoken words – 'Morning, Beau Gregory' to the dark-blue demoiselle sprinkled with bright-blue spots, the 'jewel fish' that exactly resembles the starlit fashioning of a bottle of Worth's 'Vol de Nuit'; 'Sorry. Not today, sweetheart,' to a fluttering butterfly fish with false black 'eyes' on its tail and, 'You're too fat anyway, Blue Boy,' to an indigo parrot fish that must have weighed a good ten pounds – his eyes were searching for only one of his 'people' – his only enemy on the reef, the only one he killed on sight, a scorpion fish.

Scorpion fish inhabit most of the southern waters of the world, and the 'rascasse' that is the foundation of *bouillabaisse* belongs to the family. The West Indian variety runs up to only about twelve inches long and perhaps a pound in weight. It is by far the ugliest fish in the sea, as if nature were giving warning. It is a mottled brownish grey with a heavy, wedge-shaped shaggy head. It has fleshy pendulous 'eyebrows' that droop over angry red eyes and a coloration and broken silhouette that are perfect camouflage on the reef. Though a small fish, its heavily toothed mouth is so wide that it can swallow whole most of the smaller reef fishes, but its supreme weapon lies in its erectile dorsal fins, the first few of which, acting on contact like hypodermic needles, are fed by poison glands containing enough tetrodotoxin to kill a man if they merely graze him in a vulnerable spot – in an artery, for instance, or over the heart or in the groin. They constitute the only real danger to the reef swimmer, far more dangerous than barracuda or shark, because, supremely confident in their camouflage and armoury, they flee before nothing except the very close approach of a foot or actual contact. Then they flit only a few yards on wide and bizarrely striped pectorals and settle again watchfully either on the sand, where they look like a lump of overgrown coral, or amongst the rocks and seaweed, where they virtually disappear. And Major Smythe was determined to find one, spear it and give it to his octopus to see if it would take or spurn it, see if one of the ocean's great predators would recognize the deadliness of another, know of its poison. Would the octopus consume the belly and leave the spines? Would it eat the lot and, if so, would it suffer from the poison? These were the questions Bengry at the Institute wanted answered and today, since it was going to be the beginning of the end of Major Smythe's life at Wavelets and though it might mean the end of his darling Octopussy, Major Smythe had decided to find out the answers and leave one tiny memorial to his now futile life in some dusty corner of the Institute's marine biological files.

For, only a couple of hours earlier, Major Dexter Smythe's already dismal life had changed very much for the worse. So much for the worse that he would be lucky if, in a few weeks' time – time for the sending of cables from Government House to the Colonial Office, to be relayed to the Secret Service and thence to Scotland Yard and the Public Prosecutor, and for Major Smythe's transportation to London with a police escort – he got away with a sentence of imprisonment for life.

And all this because of a man called Bond, Commander James Bond, who had turned up at ten thirty that morning in a taxi from Kingston.

The day had started normally. Major Smythe had awoken from his Secconal sleep, swallowed a couple of Panadols (his heart condition forbade him aspirin), showered and skimped his breakfast under the umbrella-shaped sea-almonds and spent an hour feeding the remains of his breakfast to the birds. He then took his prescribed doses of anti-coagulant and blood-pressure pills and killed time with the *Daily Gleaner* until he could have his elevenses which, for some months now, he had advanced to ten thirty. He had just poured himself the first of two stiff brandies and ginger ales, 'the drunkard's drink', when he heard the car coming up the drive.

Luna, his coloured housekeeper, came out into the garden and announced, 'Gemmun to see you, Major.'

'What's his name?'

'Him doan say, Major. Him say to tell you him come from Govment House.'

Major Smythe was wearing nothing but a pair of old khaki shorts and sandals. He said, 'All right, Luna. Put him in the living-room and say I won't be a moment,' and went round the back way into his bedroom and put on a white bush shirt and trousers and brushed his hair. Government House! Now what the hell?

As soon as he had walked through into the living-room and seen the tall man in the dark-blue tropical suit standing at the picture window looking out to sea, Major Smythe had somehow sensed bad news. Then, when the man had turned slowly to look at him with watchful, serious blue-grey eyes, he had known that this was officialdom, and when his cheery smile was not returned, inimical officialdom. A chill had run down Major Smythe's spine. 'They' had somehow found out.

'Well, well. I'm Smythe. I gather you're from Government House. How's Sir Kenneth?'

There was somehow no question of shaking hands. The man said, 'I haven't met him. I only arrived a couple of days ago. I've been out round the island most of the time. My name's Bond, James Bond. I'm from the Ministry of Defence.'

Major Smythe remembered the hoary euphemism for the Secret Service. He said, with forced cheerfulness, 'Oh. The old firm?'

The question had been ignored. 'Is there somewhere we can talk?'

'Rather. Anywhere you like. Here or in the garden? What about a drink?' Major Smythe clinked the ice in the glass he still held in his hand. 'Rum and ginger's the local poison. I prefer the ginger by itself.' The lie came out with the automatic smoothness of the alcoholic.

'No thanks. And here would be fine.' The man leaned negligently against the wide mahogany window-sill.

Major Smythe sat down and threw a jaunty leg over the low arm of one of the comfortable planters' chairs he had had copied from an original by the local cabinet-maker. He pulled out the drink coaster from the other arm, took a deep pull at his glass and slid it, with a consciously steady hand, down into the hole in the wood. 'Well,' he said cheerily, looking the other man straight in the eyes, 'what can I do for you? Somebody been up to some dirty work on the North Shore and you need a spare hand? Be glad to get into harness again. It's been a long time since those days, but I can still remember some of the old routines.'

'Do you mind if I smoke?' The man had already

got his cigarette case in his hand. It was a flat gun-metal one that would hold a round fifty. Somehow this small sign of a shared weakness comforted Major Smythe.

'Of course, my dear fellow.' He made a move to get up, his lighter ready.

'It's all right, thanks.' James Bond had already lit his cigarette. 'No, it's nothing local. I want to, I've been sent out to ask you to recall your work for the Service at the end of the war.' James Bond paused and looked down at Major Smythe carefully. 'Particularly the time when you were working with the Miscellaneous Objectives Bureau.'

Major Smythe laughed sharply. He had known it. He had known it for absolutely sure. But when it came out of this man's mouth, the laugh had been forced out of Major Smythe like the scream of a hit man. 'Oh Lord, yes. Good old MOB. That was a lark all right.' He laughed again. He felt the anginal pain, brought on by the pressure of what he knew was coming, build up across his chest. He dipped his hand into his trouser pocket, tilted the little bottle into the palm of his hand and slipped the white TNT pill under his tongue. He was amused to see the tension coil up in the other man, the way the eyes narrowed watchfully. It's all right, my dear fellow. This isn't a death pill. He said, 'You troubled with acidosis? No? It slays me when I go on a bender. Last night. Party at Jamaica Inn. One really ought to stop thinking one's always twenty-five. Anyway, let's get back to MOB Force. Not many of us left, I suppose.' He felt the pain across his chest withdraw into its lair. 'Something to do with the Official History?'

James Bond looked down at the tip of his cigarette. 'Not exactly.'

'I expect you know I wrote most of the chapter on the Force for the War Book. It's a long time ago now. Doubt if I'd have much to add today.'

'Nothing more about that operation in the Tyrol – place called Ober Aurach, about a mile east of Kitzbühel?'

One of the names he had been living with for all these years forced another harsh laugh out of Major Smythe. 'That was a piece of cake! You've never seen such a shambles. All those Gestapo toughs with their doxies. All of 'em hog-drunk. They'd kept their files all tickety-boo. Handed them over without a murmur. Hoped that'd earn 'em easy treatment, I suppose. We gave the stuff a first going-over and shipped all the bods off to the Munich camp. Last I heard of them. Most of them hanged for war crimes, I expect. We handed the bumph over to HQ at Salzburg. Then we went on up the Mittersill valley after another hideout.' Major Smythe took a good pull at his drink and lit a cigarette. He looked up. 'That's the long and the short of it.'

'You were Number 2 at the time, I think. The CO was an American, a Colonel King from Patton's army.'

'That's right. Nice fellow. Wore a moustache, which isn't like an American. Knew his way among the local wines. Quite a civilized chap.'

'In his report about the operation he wrote that he handed you all the documents for a preliminary run-through as you were the German expert with the unit. Then you gave them all back to him with your comments?' James Bond paused. 'Every single one of them?'

Major Smythe ignored the innuendo. 'That's right. Mostly lists of names. Counter-Intelligence dope. The CI people in Salzburg were very pleased with the stuff. Gave them plenty of new leads. I expect the originals are lying about somewhere. They'll have been used for the Nuremberg Trials. Yes, by Jove!' Major Smythe was reminiscent, pally. 'Those were some of the jolliest months of my life, haring around the country with MOB Force. Wine, women and song! And you can say that again!'

Here, Major Smythe was saying the whole truth. He had had a dangerous and uncomfortable war until 1945. When the Commandos were formed in 1941 he had volunteered and been seconded from the Royal Marines to Combined Operations Head-quarters under Mountbatten. There his excellent German (his mother had come from Heidelberg) had earned him the unenviable job of being advanced in-terrogator on Commando operations across the Channel. He had been lucky to get away from two years of this work unscathed and with the OBE

(Military), which was sparingly awarded in the last war. And then, in preparation for the defeat of Germany, the Miscellaneous Objectives Bureau had been formed jointly by the Secret Service and Combined Operations, and Major Smythe had been given the temporary rank of Lieutenant-Colonel and told to form a unit whose job would be the cleaning up of Gestapo and Abwehr hideouts when the collapse of Germany came about. The OSS got to hear of the scheme and insisted on getting into the act to cope with the American wing of the front, and the result was the creation of not one but six units that went into operation in Germany and Austria on the day of surrender. They were units of twenty men, each with a light armoured car, six jeeps, a wireless truck and three lorries, and they were controlled by a joint Anglo-American headquarters in SHAEF, which also fed them with targets from the army intelligence units and from the SIS and OSS. Major Smythe had been Number 2 of 'A' Force which had been allotted the Tyrol – an area full of good hiding places with easy access to Italy and perhaps out of Europe – that was known to have been chosen as funkhole number 1 by the people MOB Force was after. And, as Major Smythe had just told Bond, they had had themselves a ball. All without firing a shot – except that is, two fired by Major Smythe.

James Bond said casually, 'Does the name of Hannes Oberhauser ring a bell?'

Major Smythe frowned, trying to remember.

'Can't say it does.' It was eighty degrees in the shade, but he shivered.

'Let me refresh your memory. On the same day as those documents were given to you to look over, you made inquiries at the Tiefenbrunner Hotel, where you were billeted, for the best mountain guide in Kitzbühel. You were referred to Oberhauser. The next day you asked your CO for a day's leave which was granted. Early next morning you went to Oberhauser's chalet, put him under close arrest and drove him away in your jeep. Does that ring a bell?'

That phrase about 'refreshing your memory'. How often had Major Smythe himself used it when he was trying to trap a German liar? Take your time! You've been ready for something like this for years. Major Smythe shook his head doubtfully. 'Can't say it does.'

'A man with greying hair and a gammy leg. Spoke some English as he'd been a ski-instructor before the war.'

Major Smythe looked candidly into the cold, clear eyes. 'Sorry. Can't help you.'

James Bond took a small blue leather notebook out of his inside pocket and turned the leaves. He stopped turning them. He looked up. 'At that time, as sidearms, you were carrying a regulation Webley & Scott ·45 with the serial number 8967/362.'

'It was certainly a Webley. Damned clumsy weapon. Hope they've got something more like the Luger or the heavy Beretta these days. But I can't say I ever took a note of the number.'

'The number's right enough,' said James Bond. 'I've got the date of its issue to you by HQ and the date when you turned it in. You signed the book both times.'

Major Smythe shrugged. 'Well then, it must have been my gun. But' – he put rather angry impatience into his voice – 'what, if I may ask, is all this in aid of?'

James Bond looked at him almost with curiosity. He said, and now his voice was not unkind, 'You know what it's all about, Smythe.' He paused and seemed to reflect. 'Tell you what. I'll go out into the garden for ten minutes or so. Give you time to think things over. Give me a hail.' He added seriously, 'It'll make things so much easier for you if you come out with the story in your own words.' He walked to the door into the garden. He turned round. 'I'm afraid it's only a question of dotting the i's and crossing the t's. You see I had a talk with the Foo brothers in Kingston yesterday.' He stepped out on to the lawn.

Something in Major Smythe was relieved. Now at least the battle of wits, the trying to invent alibis, the evasions, were over. If this man Bond had got to the Foos, to either of them, they would have spilled the beans. The last thing they wanted was to get in bad with the government, and anyway there was only about six inches of the stuff left.

Major Smythe got briskly to his feet, went to the loaded sideboard and poured himself out another brandy and ginger ale, almost fifty-fifty. He might as well live it up while there was still time! The future

wouldn't hold many more of these for him. He went
back to his chair and lit his twentieth cigarette of the
day. He looked at his watch. It said eleven thirty. If
he could be rid of the chap in an hour, he'd have
plenty of time with his 'people'. He sat and drank and
marshalled his thoughts. He could make the story
long or short, put in the weather and the way the
flowers and pines had smelled on the mountain, or he
could cut it short. He would cut it short.

Up in that big double bedroom in the Tiefenbrunner, with the wads of buff and grey paper spread
out on the spare bed, he hadn't been looking for anything special, just taking samples here and there and
concentrating on the ones marked in red KOMMAN-
DOSACHE, HOECHST VERTRAULICH. There weren't
many of these, and they were mostly confidential
reports on German top brass, intercepts of broken
Allied cyphers and the whereabouts of secret dumps.
Since these were the main targets of 'A' Force, Major
Smythe had scanned them with particular excitement
– food, explosives, guns, espionage records, files of
Gestapo personnel – a tremendous haul! And then, at
the bottom of the packet, there had been the single
envelope sealed with red wax and the notation ONLY
TO BE OPENED IN FINAL EMERGENCY. The
envelope contained one single sheet of paper. It was
unsigned and the few words were written in red ink.
The heading said VALUTA, and beneath was written
WILDE KAISER. FRANZISKANER HALT. 100 M.
OESTLICH STEINHÜGEL. WAFFENKISTE. ZWEI

BAR 24 KT and then a list of measurements in centi-
metres. Major Smythe held his hands apart as if telling
a story about a fish he had caught. Each bar would be
nearly as big as a couple of bricks. And one single
English sovereign of only eighteen-carat was selling
nowadays for two to three pounds! This was a
bloody fortune! Forty, fifty thousand pounds' worth!
Maybe even a hundred! He had no idea, but, quite
coolly and speedily, in case anyone should come in,
he put a match to the paper and the envelope, ground
the ashes to powder and swilled them down the lava-
tory. Then he took out his large-scale Austrian Ord-
nance map of the area and in a moment had his finger
on the Franziskaner Halt. It was marked as an un-
inhabited mountaineers' refuge on a saddle just below
the highest of the easterly peaks of the Kaiser mountains, that awe-inspiring range of giant stone teeth
that give Kitzbühel its threatening northern horizon.
And the cairn of stones would be about there, his
fingernail pointed, and the whole bloody lot was
only ten miles and perhaps a five hours' climb away!

The beginning had been as this fellow Bond had
described. He had gone to Oberhauser's chalet at four
in the morning, had arrested him and had told his
weeping, protesting family that he, Smythe, was
taking him to an interrogation camp in Munich. If
the guide's record was clean, he would be back home
within a week. If the family kicked up a fuss it would
only make trouble for Oberhauser. Smythe had re-
fused to give his name and had had the forethought to

shroud the numbers on his jeep. In twenty-four hours, 'A' Force would be on its way and, by the time military government got to Kitzbühel, the incident would already be buried under the morass of the occupation tangle.

Oberhauser had been a nice enough chap once he had recovered from his fright, and when Smythe talked knowingly about skiing and climbing, both of which he had done before the war, the pair, as Smythe intended, became quite pally. Their route lay along the bottom of the Kaiser range to Kufstein, and Smythe drove slowly, making admiring comments on the peaks that were now flushed with the pink of dawn. Finally, below the Peak of Gold, as he called it to himself, he slowed to a halt and pulled off the road into a grassy glade. He turned in his seat and said candidly, 'Oberhauser, you are a man after my own heart. We share many interests together and from your talk and from the man I think you to be, I am sure you did not cooperate with the Nazis. Now I will tell you what I will do. We will spend the day climbing on the Kaiser and I will then drive you back to Kitzbühel and report to my commanding officer that you have been cleared at Munich.' He grinned cheerfully. 'Now. How about that?'

The man had been near to tears of gratitude. But could he have some kind of paper to show that he was a good citizen? Certainly. Major Smythe's signature would be quite enough. The pact was made, the jeep was driven up a track and well hidden from the road and they were off at a steady pace, climbing up through the pine-scented foot-hills.

Smythe was well dressed for the climb. He had nothing on under his bush jacket, shorts and a pair of the excellent rubber-soled boots issued to American parachutists. His only burden was the Webley & Scott and, tactfully, for Oberhauser was after all one of the enemy, Oberhauser didn't suggest that he leave it behind some conspicuous rock. Oberhauser was in his best suit and boots, but that didn't seem to bother him and he assured Major Smythe that ropes and pitons would not be needed for their climb and that there was a hut directly up above them where they could rest. It was called the Franziskaner Halt.

'Is it indeed?' said Major Smythe.

'Yes, and below it there is a small glacier. Very pretty, but we will climb round it. There are many crevasses.'

'Is that so?' said Major Smythe thoughtfully. He examined the back of Oberhauser's head, now beaded with sweat. After all, he was only a bloody Kraut, or at any rate of that ilk. What would one more or less matter? It was all going to be as easy as falling off a log. The only thing that worried Major Smythe was getting the bloody stuff down the mountain. He decided that he would somehow sling the bars across his back. After all, he could slide it most of the way in its ammunition box or whatnot.

It was a long, dreary hack up the mountain and

when they were above the tree line the sun came up and it was very hot. And now it was all rock and scree, and their long zigzags sent boulders and rubble rumbling and crashing down the slope that got ever steeper as they approached the final crag, grey and menacing, that lanced away into the blue above them. They were both naked to the waist and sweating so that the sweat ran down their legs into their boots, but, despite Oberhauser's limp, they kept up a good pace, and when they stopped for a drink and a swab down at a hurtling mountain stream Oberhauser congratulated Major Smythe on his fitness. Major Smythe, his mind full of dreams, said curtly and untruthfully that all English soldiers were fit, and they went on.

The rock face wasn't difficult. Major Smythe had known that it wouldn't be or the climbers' hut couldn't have been built on the shoulder. Toe holds had been cut in the face and there were occasional iron pegs hammered into crevices. But he couldn't have found the more difficult traverses alone and he congratulated himself on deciding to bring a guide.

Once, Oberhauser's hand, testing for a grip, dislodged a great slab of rock, loosened by years of snow and frost, and sent it crashing down the mountain. Major Smythe suddenly thought about noise. 'Many people around here?' he asked as they watched the boulder hurtle down into the tree line.

'Not a soul until you get near Kufstein,' said Oberhauser. He gestured along the arid range of high peaks. 'No grazing. Little water. Only the climbers come here. And since the beginning of the war . . .' He left the phrase unfinished.

They skirted the blue-fanged glacier below the final climb to the shoulder. Major Smythe's careful eyes took in the width and depth of the crevasses. Yes, they would fit! Directly above them, perhaps a hundred feet up under the lee of the shoulder, were the weather-beaten boards of the hut. Major Smythe measured the angle of the slope. Yes, it was almost a straight dive down. Now or later? He guessed later. The line of the last traverse wasn't very clear.

They were up at the hut in five hours flat. Major Smythe said he wanted to relieve himself and wandered casually along the shoulder to the east, paying no heed to the beautiful panoramas of Austria and Bavaria that stretched away on either side of him perhaps fifty miles into the heat haze. He counted his paces carefully. At exactly 120 there was the cairn of stones, a loving memorial, perhaps, to some long-dead climber. Major Smythe, knowing differently, longed to tear it apart there and then. Instead he took out his Webley & Scott, squinted down the barrel and twirled the cylinder. Then he walked back.

It was cold up there at ten thousand feet or more, and Oberhauser had got into the hut and was busy preparing a fire. Major Smythe controlled his horror at the sight. 'Oberhauser,' he said cheerfully, 'come out and show me some of the sights. Wonderful view up here.'

'Certainly, Major.' Oberhauser followed Major Smythe out of the hut. Outside he fished in his hip pocket and produced something wrapped in paper. He undid the paper to reveal a hard, wrinkled sausage. He offered it to the Major. 'It is only what we call a "Soldat",' he said shyly. 'Smoked meat. Very tough but good.' He smiled. 'It is like what they eat in Wild West films. What is the name?'

' "Biltong",' said the Major. Then – and later this had slightly disgusted him – he said, 'Leave it in the hut. We will share it later. Come over here. Can we see Innsbruck? Show me the view on this side.'

Oberhauser bobbed into the hut and out again. The Major fell in just behind him as he talked, pointing out this or that distant church spire or mountain peak.

They came to the point above the glacier. Major Smythe drew his revolver and, at a range of two feet, fired two bullets into the base of Hannes Oberhauser's skull. No muffing! Dead on!

The impact of the bullets knocked the guide clean off his feet and over the edge. Major Smythe craned over. The body hit twice only and then crashed on to the glacier. But not on to its fissured origin. Half-way down and on a patch of old snow! 'Hell!' said Major Smythe.

The deep boom of the two shots that had been batting to and fro among the mountains died away. Major Smythe took one last look at the black splash on the white snow and hurried off along the shoulder. First things first!

He started on the top of the cairn, working as if the devil was after him, throwing the rough, heavy stones indiscriminately down the mountain to right or left. His hands began to bleed, but he hardly noticed. Now there were only two feet or so left, and nothing! Bloody nothing! He bent to the last pile, scrabbling feverishly. And then! Yes! The edge of a metal box. A few more rocks away and there was the whole of it! A good old grey Wehrmacht ammunition box with the trace of some lettering still on it. Major Smythe gave a groan of joy. He sat down on a hard piece of rock and his mind went orbiting through Bentleys, Monte Carlo, pent-house flats, Cartier's, champagne, caviare and, incongruously, but because he loved golf, a new set of Henry Cotton irons.

Drunk with his dreams, Major Smythe sat there looking at the grey box for a full quarter of an hour. Then he glanced at his watch and got briskly to his feet. Time to get rid of the evidence. The box had a handle at each end. Major Smythe had expected it to be heavy. He had mentally compared its probable weight with the heaviest thing he had ever carried – a forty-pound salmon he had caught in Scotland just before the war – but the box was more than double that weight, and he was only just able to heave it out of its last bed of rocks on to the thin alpine grass. He slung his handkerchief through one of the handles and dragged it clumsily along the shoulder to the hut. Then he sat down on the stone doorstep, and, his eyes never leaving the box, tore at Oberhauser's smoked sausage with his strong teeth and thought about getting his fifty thousand pounds – for that was the figure he put it at – down the mountain and into a new hiding place.

Oberhauser's sausage was a real mountaineer's meal – tough, well fatted and strongly garlicked. Bits of it stuck uncomfortably between Major Smythe's teeth. He dug them out with a sliver of matchstick and spat them on the ground. Then his intelligence-wise mind came into operation and he meticulously searched among the stones and grass, picked up the scraps and swallowed them. From now on he was a criminal – as much a criminal as if he had robbed a bank and shot the guard. He was a cop turned robber. He *must* remember that! It would be death if he didn't – death instead of Cartier's. All he had to do was to take infinite pains. He would take those pains, and by God they would be infinite! Then, for ever after, he would be rich and happy. After taking ridiculously minute trouble to eradicate any sign of entry into the hut, he dragged the ammunition box to the edge of the last rock face and, aiming it away from the glacier, tipped it, with a prayer, into space.

The grey box, turning slowly in the air, hit the first steep slope below the rock face, bounded another hundred feet and landed with an iron clang in some loose scree and stopped. Major Smythe couldn't see if it had burst open. He didn't mind one way or the other. The mountain might as well do it for him!

With a last look round, he went over the edge. He took great care at each piton, tested every handhold and foothold before he put weight on them. Coming down, he was a much more valuable life than he had been climbing up. He made for the glacier and trudged across the melting snow to the black patch on the icefield. There was nothing to be done about footprints. It would only take a few days for them to be melted down by the sun. He got to the body. He had seen many corpses during the war, and the blood and broken limbs meant nothing to him. He dragged the remains of Oberhauser to the nearest deep crevasse and toppled it in. Then he went carefully round the lip of the crevasse and kicked the snow overhang down on top of the body. Satisfied with his work, he retraced his steps, placing his feet exactly in his old footprints, and made his way on down the slope to the ammunition box.

Yes, the mountain had burst open the lid for him. Almost casually he tore away the cartridge-paper wrappings. The two great hunks of metal glittered up at him under the sun. There were the same markings on each – the swastika in a circle below an eagle, and the date, 1943 – the mint marks of the Reichsbank. Major Smythe gave a nod of approval. He replaced the paper and hammered the crooked lid half-shut with a rock. Then he tied the lanyard of his Webley round one of the handles and moved on down the mountain, dragging his clumsy burden behind him.

It was now one o'clock and the sun beat fiercely down on his naked chest, frying him in his own sweat. His reddened shoulders began to burn. So did his face. To hell with them! He stopped at the stream from the glacier, dipped his handkerchief in the water and tied it across his forehead. Then he drank deeply and went on, occasionally cursing the ammunition box as it caught up with him and banged at his heels. But these discomforts, the sunburn and the bruises, were nothing compared with what he would have to face when he got down to the valley and the going levelled out. For the time being he had gravity on his side. There would come at least a mile when he would have to carry the blasted stuff. Major Smythe winced at the thought of the havoc it would wreak on his burned back. 'Oh well,' he said to himself almost light-headedly, 'il faut souffrir pour être millionaire!'

When he got to the bottom and the time had come he sat and rested on a mossy bank under the firs. Then he spread out his bush shirt and heaved the two bars out of the box and on to its centre, tying the tails of the shirt as firmly as he could to where the sleeves sprang from the shoulders. After digging a shallow hole in the bank and burying the empty box, he knotted the two cuffs of the sleeves firmly together, knelt down and slipped his head through the rough sling, got his hands on either side of the knot to protect his neck, and staggered to his feet, crouching far forward so as not to be pulled over on his back.

Then, crushed under half his own weight, his back on fire under the contact with his burden, and his breath rasping through his constricted lungs, coolie-like, he shuffled slowly off down the little path through the trees.

To this day he didn't know how he had made it to the jeep. Again and again the knots gave under the strain and the bars crashed down on the calves of his legs, and each time he had sat with his head in his hands and then started all over again. But finally, by concentrating on counting his steps and stopping for a rest at every hundredth, he got to the blessed little car and collapsed beside it. And then there had been the business of burying his hoard in the wood, amongst a jumble of big rocks that he would be sure to find again, and of cleaning himself up as best he could and getting back to his billet by a circuitous route that avoided the Oberhauser chalet. And then it was all done and he had got drunk by himself on a bottle of cheap schnapps, eaten and gone to bed and to a stupefied sleep. The next day, MOB 'A' Force had moved off up the Mittersill valley on a fresh trail, and six months later Major Smythe was back in London and his war was over.

But not his problems. Gold is difficult stuff to smuggle, certainly in the quantity available to Major Smythe, and it was now essential to get his two bars across the Channel and into a new hiding place. So he put off his demobilization and clung to the privileges of his temporary rank, particularly to his

Military Intelligence passes, and soon got himself sent back to Germany as a British representative at the Combined Interrogation Centre in Munich. There he did a scratch job for six months during which he collected his gold and stowed it away in a battered suitcase in his quarters. Then on two week-end leaves he flew to England, each time carrying one of the bars in a bulky briefcase. The walk across the tarmac at Munich and Northolt and the handling of his case as if it contained only papers required two benzedrine tablets and a will of iron; but at last he had his fortune safe in the basement of an aunt's flat in Kensington and could get on with the next phase of his plans at leisure. He resigned from the Royal Marines, got himself demobilized and married one of the many girls he had slept with at MOB Force Headquarters, a charming blonde Wren called Mary Parnell from a solid middle-class family. He got passages for them both in one of the early banana boats sailing from Avonmouth to Kingston, Jamaica, which they both agreed would be a paradise of sunshine, good food and cheap drink and a glorious haven from the gloom, restrictions and Labour Government of postwar England. Before they sailed, Major Smythe showed Mary the gold bars, from which he had chiselled away the mint marks of the Reichsbank. 'I've been clever, darling,' he said. 'I just don't trust the pound these days, so I've sold out all my securities and swapped the lot for gold. There'll be over twenty thousand pounds' worth there if I play it right. That should give us a fair slice of the good life, just cutting off a chunk now and then and selling it.'

Mary Parnell was not familiar with the ramifications of the currency laws. She knelt down and ran her hands lovingly over the gleaming bars. Then she got up and threw her arms round Major Smythe's neck and kissed him. 'You're a wonderful, wonderful man,' she said, almost in tears. 'Frightfully clever and handsome and brave and now you're rich as well. I'm the luckiest girl in the world.'

'Well anyway we're rich,' said Major Smythe. 'But promise me you won't breathe a word or we'll have all the burglars in Jamaica round our ears. Promise?'

'Cross my heart.'

Prince's Club, in the foot-hills above Kingston, was indeed a paradise. Pleasant enough members, wonderful servants, unlimited food and cheap drink, and all in the wonderful setting of the tropics that neither of them had known before. They were a popular couple and Major Smythe's war record earned them the entrée to Government House society, after which their life was one endless round of parties, with tennis for Mary and golf (with the Henry Cotton irons!) for Major Smythe. In the evenings there was bridge for her and the high poker game for him. Yes, it was paradise all right, while, in their homeland, people munched their spam, fiddled in the black market, cursed the government and suffered the worst winter weather for thirty years.

The Smythes met all their initial expenditure from their combined cash reserves, swollen by wartime gratuities, and it took Major Smythe a full year of careful sniffing around before he decided to do business with the Messrs Foo, import and export merchants. The brothers Foo, highly respected and very rich, were the acknowledged governing junta of the flourishing Chinese community in Jamaica. Some of their trading was suspected to be devious in the Chinese tradition, but all Major Smythe's casually meticulous inquiries confirmed that they were utterly trustworthy. The Bretton Woods Convention, fixing a controlled world price for gold, had been signed and it had already become common knowledge that in Tangier and Macao – two free ports which, for different reasons, had escaped the Bretton Woods net – a price of at least one hundred dollars per ounce of gold, ninety-nine fine, could be obtained compared with the fixed world price of thirty-five dollars per ounce. And, conveniently, the Foos had just begun to trade again with a resurgent Hong Kong, already the entrepôt for gold-smuggling into the neighbouring Macao. The whole set-up was, in Major Smythe's language, tickety-boo. He had a most pleasant meeting with the Foo brothers. No questions were asked until it came to examining the bars. At this point the absence of mint marks resulted in a polite inquiry as to the original provenance of the gold.

'You see, Major,' said the older and blander of the brothers behind the big, empty, mahogany desk, 'in the bullion market the mint marks of all respectable national banks and responsible dealers are accepted without question. Such marks guarantee the fineness of the gold. But of course there are other banks and dealers whose methods of refining,' his benign smile widened a fraction, 'are perhaps not quite, shall we say, so accurate.'

'You mean the old gold brick swindle,' said Major Smythe with a twinge of anxiety. 'Hunk of lead covered with gold plating?'

Both brothers tee-heed reassuringly. 'No, no, Major. That of course is out of the question. But,' the smiles held constant, 'if you cannot recall the provenance of these fine bars, perhaps you would have no objection if we were to undertake an assay. There are methods of determining the exact fineness of such bars. My brother and I are competent in these methods. If you would care to leave these with us and perhaps come back after lunch?'

There had been no alternative. Major Smythe had to trust the Foos utterly now. They could cook up any figure and he would just have to accept it. He went over to the Myrtle Bank and had one or two stiff drinks and a sandwich that stuck in his throat. Then he went back to the cool office of the Foos.

The setting was the same – the two smiling brothers, the two bars of gold, the briefcase, but now there was a piece of paper and a gold Parker pen in front of the elder brother.

'We have solved the problem of your fine bars, Major,' ('Fine'! Thank God, thought Major Smythe) 'and I am sure you will be interested to know their probable history.'

'Yes indeed,' said Major Smythe, with a brave show of enthusiasm.

'They are German bars, Major. Probably from the wartime Reichsbank. This we have deduced from the fact that they contain ten per cent of lead. Under the Hitler régime, it was the foolish habit of the Reichsbank to adulterate their gold in this manner. This fact became rapidly known to dealers and the price of German bars, in Switzerland, for instance, where many of them found their way, was adjusted downwards accordingly. So the only result of the German foolishness was that the national bank of Germany lost a reputation for honest dealing it had earned over the centuries.' The Chinaman's smile didn't vary. 'Very bad business, Major. Very stupid.'

Major Smythe marvelled at the omniscience of these two men so far from the great commercial channels of the world, but he also cursed it. Now what? He said, 'That's very interesting, Mr Foo. But it is not very good news for me. Are these bars not "good delivery", or whatever you call it in the bullion world?'

The elder Foo made a slight throwaway gesture with his right hand. 'It is of no importance, Major.

Or rather, it is of very small importance. We will sell your gold at its true mint value, let us say, eighty-nine fine. It may be re-fined by the ultimate purchaser, or it may not. That is not our business. We shall have sold a true bill of goods.'

'But at a lower price.'

'That is so, Major. But I think I have some good news for you. Have you any estimates as to the worth of these two bars?'

'I had thought around twenty thousand pounds.'

The elder Foo gave a dry chuckle. 'I think, if we sell wisely and slowly, you should receive more than one hundred thousand dollars, Major – subject, that is, to our commission, which will include shipping and incidental charges.'

'How much would that be?'

'We were thinking about a figure of ten per cent, Major. If that is satisfactory to you.'

Major Smythe had an idea that bullion brokers received a fraction of one per cent. But what the hell? He had already as good as made ten thousand pounds since lunch. He said 'Done' and got up and reached his hand across the desk.

From then on, every quarter, he would visit the office of the Foos, carrying an empty suitcase. There would be five hundred new Jamaican pounds in neat bundles on the broad desk and the two gold bars, that diminished inch by inch, together with a typed slip showing the amount sold and the price obtained in Macao. It was all very simple and friendly and highly businesslike, and Major Smythe didn't think that he was being submitted to any form of squeeze other than the duly recorded ten per cent. In any case he didn't particularly care. Two thousand net a year was good enough for him, and his only worry was that the income tax people would get after him and ask him what he was living on. He mentioned this possibility to the Foos. But they said he was not to worry and, for the next two quarters, there was only four hundred pounds instead of five on the table and no comment was made by either side. 'Squeeze' had been administered in the right quarter.

And so the lazy, sunshiny days passed by and stretched out into years. The Smythes both put on weight and Major Smythe had the first of his two coronaries and was told by his doctor to cut down on his alcohol and cigarettes and take life more easily. He was also to avoid fats and fried food. At first Mary Smythe tried to be firm with him; then, when he took to secret drinking and to a life of petty lies and evasions, she tried to back-pedal on her attempts to control his self-indulgence. But she was too late. She had already become the symbol of the janitor to Major Smythe and he took to avoiding her. She berated him with not loving her any more and, when the resultant bickering became too much for her simple nature, she became a sleeping-pill addict. Then, after one flaming, drunken row, she took an overdose 'just to show him'. It was too much of an overdose and it killed her. The suicide was hushed up, but the resultant cloud did Major Smythe no good socially and he returned to the North Shore which, although only some three miles across the island from the capital, is, even in the small society of Jamaica, a different world. And there he had settled in Wavelets and, after his second coronary, was in the process of drinking himself to death when this man called Bond arrived on the scene with an alternative death warrant in his pocket.

Major Smythe looked at his watch. It was a few minutes after twelve o'clock. He got up and poured himself another stiff brandy and ginger ale and went out on to the lawn. James Bond was sitting under the sea-almonds, gazing out to sea. He didn't look up when Major Smythe pulled up another aluminium garden chair and put his drink on the grass beside him. When Major Smythe had finished telling his story, Bond said unemotionally, 'Yes, that's more or less the way I figured it.'

'Want me to write it all out and sign it?'

'You can if you like. But not for me. That'll be for the court martial. Your old Corps will be handling all that. I've got nothing to do with the legal aspects. I shall put in a report to my own Service of what you've told me and they'll pass it on to the Royal Marines. Then I suppose it'll go to the Public Prosecutor via Scotland Yard.'

'Could I ask a question?'

'Of course.'

'How did they find out?'

'It was a small glacier. Oberhauser's body came out at the bottom of it earlier this year. When the spring snows melted. Some climbers found it. All his papers and everything were intact. The family identified him. Then it was just a question of working back. The bullets clinched it.'

'But how did you get mixed up in the whole thing?'

'MOB Force was a responsibility of my, er, Service. The papers found their way to us. I happened to see the file. I had some spare time on my hands. I asked to be given the job of chasing up the man who did it.'

'Why?'

James Bond looked Major Smythe squarely in the eyes. 'It just happened that Oberhauser was a friend of mine. He taught me to ski before the war, when I was in my teens. He was a wonderful man. He was something of a father to me at a time when I happened to need one.'

'Oh, I see.' Major Smythe looked away. 'I'm sorry.'

James Bond got to his feet. 'Well, I'll be getting back to Kingston.' He held up a hand. 'No, don't bother. I'll find my way to the car.' He looked down at the older man. He said abruptly, almost harshly – perhaps, Major Smythe thought, to hide his embarrassment – 'It'll be about a week before they send someone out to bring you home.' Then he walked off across the lawn and through the house and Major Smythe heard the iron whirr of the self-starter and the clatter of the gravel on the unkempt drive.

Major Smythe, questing for his prey along the reef,
wondered what exactly those last words of the Bond
man had meant. Inside the Pirelli his lips drew mirth-
lessly back from the stained teeth. It was obvious,
really. It was just a version of the corny old act of
leaving the guilty officer alone with his revolver. If
the Bond man had wanted to, he could have tele-
phoned Government House and had an officer of the
Jamaica Regiment sent over to take Major Smythe
into custody. Decent of him, in a way. Or was it?
A suicide would be much tidier, save a lot of paper-
work and tax-payers' money. Should he oblige the
Bond man and be tidy? Join Mary in whatever place
suicides go to? Or go through with it – the indignity,
the dreary formalities, the headlines, the boredom
and drabness of a life sentence that would inevitably
end with his third coronary? Or should he defend
himself – plead wartime, a struggle with Oberhauser
on the Peak of Gold, prisoner trying to escape, Oberhauser knowing of the gold cache, the natural temp-
tation of Smythe to make away with the bullion, he,
a poor officer of the Commandos confronted with
sudden wealth? Should he dramatically throw himself on the mercy of the court? Suddenly Major
Smythe saw himself in the dock, a splendid, upright
figure, in the fine bemedalled blue and scarlet of the
ceremonial uniform which was the traditional rig for

courts martial. (Had the moths got into the japanned
box in the spare room at Wavelets? Had the damp?
Luna would have to look to it. A day in the sunshine
if the weather held. A good brushing. With the help
of his corset, he could surely still get his forty-inch
waist into the thirty-four-inch trousers Gieves had
built for him twenty, thirty years ago.) And, down
on the floor of the court, at Chatham probably, the
Prisoners' Friend, some staunch fellow, at least of
colonel's rank in deference to his own seniority,
would be pleading his cause. And there was always
the possibility of appeal to a higher court. Why, the
whole affair might become a *cause célèbre*. He would
sell his story to the papers, write a book ... Major
Smythe felt the excitement mounting in him. Careful, old boy! Careful! Remember what the good old
snip-cock had said! He put his feet to the ground
and had a rest amidst the dancing waves of the nor'-
east trades that kept the North Shore so delightfully
cool until the torrid months, August, September,
October, of the hurricane season. After his two pink
gins, skimpy lunch and happily sodden siesta, he
would have to give all this more careful thought.
And then there were cocktails with the Arundels and
dinner at the Shaw Park Beach Club with the Mar-
chesis. Then some high bridge and home to his
Secconal sleep. Cheered by the prospect of the familiar routine, the black shadow of Bond retreated into
the background. Now then, scorp, where are you?
Octopussy's waiting for her lunch! Major Smythe

put his head down and, his mind freshly focused and his eyes questing, continued his leisurely swim along the shallow valley between the coral clumps that led out towards the white-fringed reef.

Almost at once he saw the two spiny antennae of a lobster, or rather of its cousin, the West Indian langouste, weaving inquisitively towards him, towards the turbulence he was creating, from a deep fissure under a nigger-head. From the thickness of the antennae it would be a big one, three or four pounds! Normally, Major Smythe would have put his feet down and delicately stirred up the sand in front of the lair to bring the lobster farther out, for they are an inquisitive family. Then he would have speared it through the head and taken it back for lunch. But today there was only one prey in his mind, one shape to concentrate on – the shaggy, irregular silhouette of a scorpion fish. And ten minutes later, he saw a clump of seaweedy rock on the white sand that just wasn't a clump of seaweedy rock. He put his feet softly down and watched the poison spines erect themselves along the back of the thing. It was a good-sized one, perhaps three-quarters of a pound. He got his three-pronged spear ready and inched forward. Now the red angry eyes of the fish were wide open and watching him. He would have to make a single quick lunge from as nearly the vertical as possible, otherwise, he knew from experience, the barbed prongs, needle sharp though they were, would almost certainly bounce off the horny head of the beast. He swung his feet up off the ground and paddled forward very slowly, using his free hand as a fin. Now! He lunged forwards and downwards. But the scorpion fish had felt the tiny approaching shock-wave of the spear. There was a flurry of sand and it had shot up in a vertical take-off and whirred, in almost bird-like flight, under Major Smythe's belly.

Major Smythe cursed and twisted round in the water. Yes, it had done what they so often do, gone for refuge to the nearest algae-covered rock and there, confident in its superb camouflage, gone to ground on the seaweed. Major Smythe had only to swim a few feet, lunge down again, this time more accurately, and he had it, flapping and squirming on the end of his spear.

The excitement and the small exertion had caused Major Smythe to pant and he felt the old pain across his chest lurking, ready to come at him. He put his feet down and, after driving his spear all the way through the fish, held it, still flapping desperately, out of the water. Then he slowly made his way back across the lagoon on foot and walked up the sand of his beach to the wooden bench under the sea-grape. Then he dropped the spear with its jerking quarry on the sand beside him and sat down to rest.

It was perhaps five minutes later that Major Smythe felt a curious numbness more or less in the region of his solar plexus. He looked casually down and his whole body stiffened with horror and disbelief. A patch of his skin, about the size of a cricket ball, had turned white under his tan and, in the centre of the patch, there were three descending punctures topped by little beads of blood. Automatically, Major Smythe wiped away the blood. The holes were only the size of pinpricks, but Major Smythe remembered the rising flight of the scorpion fish and he said aloud, with awe in his voice, but without animosity, 'You got me, you bastard! By God, you got me!'

He sat very still, looking down at his body and remembering what it said about scorpion fish stings in the book he had borrowed from the Institute and had never returned – *Dangerous Marine Animals*, an American publication. He delicately touched and then prodded the white area round the punctures. Yes, the skin had gone totally numb and now a pulse of pain began to throb beneath it. Very soon this would become a shooting pain. Then the pain would begin to lance all over his body and become so intense that he would throw himself on the sand, screaming and thrashing about, to rid himself of it. He would vomit and foam at the mouth and then delirium and convulsions would take over until he lost consciousness. Then, inevitably in his case, there would ensue cardiac failure and death. According to the book the whole cycle would be complete in about a quarter of an hour – that was all he had left – fifteen minutes of hideous agony! There were cures, of course – procaine, antibiotics and anti-histamines – if his weak heart would stand them. But they had to be near at hand and, even if he could climb the steps up to the house and supposing Jimmy Greaves had these modern drugs, the doctor couldn't possibly get to Wavelets in under an hour.

The first jet of pain seared into Major Smythe's body and bent him over double. Then came another and another, radiating through his stomach and limbs. Now there was a dry, metallic taste in his mouth and his lips were prickling. He gave a groan and toppled off the seat on to the beach. A flapping on the sand beside his head reminded him of the scorpion fish. There came a lull in the spasms of pain. Instead his whole body felt as if it was on fire but, beneath the agony, his brain cleared. But of course! The experiment! Somehow, somehow he must get out to Octopussy and give her her lunch!

'Oh, Pussy, my Pussy, this is the last meal you'll get.'

Major Smythe mouthed the jingle to himself as he crouched on all fours, found his mask and somehow forced it over his face. Then he got hold of his spear, tipped with the still flapping fish, and, clutching his stomach with his free hand, crawled and slithered down the sand and into the water.

It was fifty yards of shallow water to the lair of the octopus in the coral cranny and Major Smythe, screaming all the while into his mask, somehow, mostly on his knees, made it. As he came to the last approach and the water became deeper, he had to get to his feet and the pain made him jiggle to and fro, as if he was a puppet manipulated by strings. Then he was there and, with a supreme effort of will, held himself steady as he dipped his head down to let some water into his mask and clear the mist of his screams from the glass. Then, blood pouring from his bitten lower lip, he bent carefully down to look into Octopussy's house. Yes! the brown mass was still there. It was stirring excitedly. Why? Major Smythe saw the dark strings of his blood curling lazily down through the water. Of course! The darling was tasting his blood. A shaft of pain hit Major Smythe and sent him reeling. He heard himself babbling deliriously into his mask. Pull yourself together, Dexter, old boy! You've got to give Pussy her lunch! He steadied himself and, holding the spear well down the shaft, lowered the fish down towards the writhing hole.

Would Pussy take the bait, the poisoned bait that was killing Major Smythe, but to which an octopus might be immune? If only Bengry could be here to watch! Three tentacles, weaving excitedly, came out of the hole and wavered round the scorpion fish. Now there was a grey mist in front of Major Smythe's eyes. He recognized it as the edge of unconsciousness and feebly shook his head to clear it. And then the tentacles leapt! But not at the fish! At Major Smythe's hand and arm. Major Smythe's torn mouth stretched in a grimace of pleasure. Now he and Pussy had shaken hands! How exciting! How truly wonderful!

But then the octopus, quietly, relentlessly, pulled

downwards and terrible realization came to Major Smythe. He summoned his dregs of strength and plunged his spear down. The only effect was to push the scorpion fish into the mass of the octopus and offer more arm to the octopus. The tentacles snaked upwards and pulled more relentlessly. Too late Major Smythe scrabbled away his mask. One bottled scream burst out across the empty bay, then his head went under and down and there was an explosion of bubbles to the surface. Then Major Smythe's legs came up and the small waves washed his body to and fro while the octopus explored his right hand with its buccal orifice and took a first tentative bite at a finger with its beak-like jaws.

The body was found by two young Jamaicans spinning for needle fish from a canoe. They speared the octopus with Major Smythe's spear, killed it in the traditional fashion by turning it inside out and biting its head off, and brought the three corpses home. They turned Major Smythe's body over to the police and had the scorpion fish and the 'sea-cat' for supper. The local correspondent of the *Daily Gleaner* reported that Major Smythe had been killed by an octopus, but the paper translated this into 'found drowned' so as not to frighten the tourists.

Later, in London, James Bond, privately assuming 'suicide', wrote the same verdict of 'found drowned', together with the date, on the last page and closed the bulky file.

It is only from the notes of Dr Greaves, who performed the autopsy, that it has been possible to construct some kind of a postscript to the bizarre and pathetic end of a once valuable officer of the Secret Service.

The Property of a Lady

I T WAS, EXCEPTIONALLY, a hot day in early June.
James Bond put down the dark grey chalk pencil
that was the marker for the dockets routed to the
double O Section and took off his coat. He didn't
bother to hang it over the back of his chair, let alone
take the trouble to get up and drape the coat over the
hanger Mary Goodnight had suspended, at her own
cost (damn women!), behind the Office of Works'
green door of his connecting office. He dropped the
coat on the floor. There was no reason to keep the
coat immaculate, the creases tidy. There was no sign
of any work to be done. All over the world there was
quiet. The In and Out signals had, for weeks, been
routine. The daily top secret SITREP, even the newspapers, yawned vacuously – in the latter case
scratchings at domestic scandals for readership, for
bad news, the only news that makes such sheets
readable, whether top secret or on sale for pennies.

Bond hated these periods of vacuum. His eyes, his
mind, were barely in focus as he turned the pages of a
jaw-breaking dissertation by the Scientific Research
Section on the Russian use of cyanide gas, propelled
by the cheapest bulb-handled children's water pistol,
for assassination. The spray, it seemed, directed at the
face, took instantaneous effect. It was recommended
for victims from twenty-five years upwards, on
ascending stairways or inclines. The verdict would
then probably be heart-failure.

The harsh burr of the red telephone sprayed into the room so suddenly that James Bond, his mind elsewhere, reached his hand automatically towards his left arm-pit in self-defence. The edges of his mouth turned down as he recognized the reflex. On the second burr he picked up the receiver.

'Sir?'

'Sir.'

He got up from his chair and picked up his coat. He put on the coat and at the same time put on his mind. He had been dozing in his bunk. Now he had to go up on the bridge. He walked through into the connecting office and resisted the impulse to ruffle up the inviting nape of Mary Goodnight's golden neck.

He told her 'M' and walked out into the close-carpeted corridor and along, between the muted whizz and zing of the Communications Section, of which his Section was a neighbour, to the lift and up to the eighth.

Miss Moneypenny's expression conveyed nothing. It usually conveyed something if she knew something – private excitement, curiosity, or, if Bond was in trouble, encouragement or even anger. Now the smile of welcome showed disinterest. Bond registered that this was going to be some kind of a routine job, a bore, and he adjusted his entrance through that fateful door accordingly.

There was a visitor – a stranger. He sat on M's left. He only briefly glanced up as Bond came in and took his usual place across the red leather-topped desk.

M said, stiffly, 'Dr Fanshawe, I don't think you've met Commander Bond of my Research Department.'

Bond was used to these euphemisms.

He got up and held out his hand. Dr Fanshawe rose, briefly touched Bond's hand and sat quickly down as if he had touched paws with a Gila monster.

If he looked at Bond, inspected him and took him in as anything more than an anatomical silhouette, Bond thought that Dr Fanshawe's eyes must be fitted with a thousandth of a second shutter. So this was obviously some kind of an expert – a man whose interests lay in facts, things, theories – not in human beings. Bond wished that M had given him some kind of a brief, hadn't got this puckish, rather childishly malign desire to surprise – to spring the jack-in-a-box on his staff. But Bond, remembering his own boredom of ten minutes ago, and putting himself in M's place, had the intuition to realize that M himself might have been subject to the same June heat, the same oppressive vacuum in his duties, and, faced by the unexpected relief of an emergency, a small one perhaps, had decided to extract the maximum effect, the maximum drama, out of it to relieve his own tedium.

The stranger was middle-aged, rosy, well-fed, and clothed rather foppishly in the neo-Edwardian fashion – turned-up cuffs to his dark blue, four-buttoned coat, a pearl pin in a heavy silk cravat, spotless wing collar, cuff links formed of what appeared to be antique coins, pince-nez on a thick black ribbon. Bond summed him up as something literary, a critic perhaps, a bachelor – possibly with homosexual tendencies.

M said, 'Dr Fanshawe is a noted authority on antique jewellery. He is also, though this is confidential, adviser to HM Customs and to the CID on such things. He has in fact been referred to me by our friends at MI5. It is in connexion with our Miss Freudenstein.'

Bond raised his eyebrows. Maria Freudenstein was a secret agent working for the Soviet KGB in the heart of the Secret Service. She was in the Communications Department, but in a watertight compartment of it that had been created especially for her, and her duties were confined to operating the Purple Cipher – a cipher which had also been created especially for her. Six times a day she was responsible for encoding and dispatching lengthy SITREPS in this cipher to the CIA in Washington. These messages were the output of Section 100 which was responsible for running double agents. They were an ingenious mixture of true fact, harmless disclosures and an occasional nugget of the grossest misinformation. Maria Freudenstein, who had been known to be a Soviet agent when she was taken into the Service, had been allowed to steal the key to the Purple Cipher with the intention that the Russians should have complete access to these SITREPS – be able to inter-

cept and decipher them – and thus, when appropriate,
be fed false information. It was a highly secret
operation which needed to be handled with extreme
delicacy, but it had now been running smoothly for
three years and, if Maria Freudenstein also picked up
a certain amount of canteen gossip at Headquarters,
that was a necessary risk, and she was not attractive
enough to form liaisons which could be a security
risk.

M turned to Dr Fanshawe. 'Perhaps, Doctor, you
would care to tell Commander Bond what it is all
about.'

'Certainly, certainly.' Dr Fanshawe looked quickly
at Bond and then away again. He addressed his boots.
'You see, it's like this, er, Commander. You've
heard of a man called Fabergé, no doubt. Famous
Russian jeweller.'

'Made fabulous Easter eggs for the Czar and Czar-
ina before the revolution.'

'That was indeed one of his specialities. He made
many other exquisite pieces of what we may broadly
describe as objects of vertu. Today, in the sale rooms,
the best examples fetch truly fabulous prices – £50,000
and more. And recently there entered this country
the most amazing specimen of all – the so-called
Emerald Sphere, a work of supreme art hitherto
known only from a sketch by the great man himself.
This treasure arrived by registered post from Paris
and it was addressed to this woman of whom you
know, Miss Maria Freudenstein.'

'Nice little present. Might I ask how you learned of it, Doctor?'

'I am, as your Chief has told you, an adviser to HM Customs and Excise in matters concerning antique jewellery and similar works of art. The declared value of the package was £100,000. This was unusual. There are methods of opening such packages clandestinely. The package was opened – under a Home Office Warrant, of course – and I was called in to examine the contents and give a valuation. I immediately recognized the Emerald Sphere from the account and sketch of it given in Mr Kenneth Snowman's definitive work on Fabergé. I said that the declared price might well be on the low side. But what I found of particular interest was the accompanying document which gave, in Russian and French, the provenance of this priceless object.' Dr Fanshawe gestured towards a photostat of what appeared to be a brief family tree that lay on the desk in front of M. 'That is a copy I had made. Briefly, it states that the Sphere was commissioned by Miss Freudenstein's grandfather directly from Fabergé in 1917 – no doubt as a means of turning some of his roubles into something portable and of great value. On his death in 1918 it passed to his brother and thence, in 1950, to Miss Freudenstein's mother. She, it appears, left Russia as a child and lived in White Russian *émigré* circles in Paris. She never married, but gave birth to this girl, Maria, illegitimately. It seems that she died last year and that some friend or executor, the paper is not signed, has now forwarded the Sphere to its rightful owner, Miss Maria Freudenstein. I had no reason to question this girl, although as you can imagine my interest was most lively, until last month Sotheby's announced that they would auction the piece, described as "the property of a lady", in a week from today. On behalf of the British Museum and, er, other interested parties, I then made discreet inquiries and met the lady, who, with perfect composure, confirmed the rather unlikely story contained in the provenance. It was then that I learned that she worked for the Ministry of Defence and it crossed my rather suspicious mind that it was, to say the least of it, odd that a junior clerk, engaged presumably on sensitive duties, should suddenly receive a gift to the value of £100,000 or more from abroad. I spoke to a senior official in MI5 with whom I have some contact through my work for HM Customs and I was in due course referred to this, er, department.' Dr Fanshawe spread his hands and gave Bond a brief glance, 'And that, Commander, is all I have to tell you.'

M broke in, 'Thank you, Doctor. Just one or two final questions and I won't detain you any further. You have examined this emerald ball thing and you pronounce it genuine?'

Dr Fanshawe ceased gazing at his boots. He looked up and spoke to a point somewhere above M's left shoulder. 'Certainly. So does Mr Snowman of Wartski's, the greatest Fabergé experts and dealers in the world. It is undoubtedly the missing master-piece of which hitherto Carl Fabergé's sketch was the only record.'

'What about the provenance? What do the experts say about that?'

'It stands up adequately. The greatest Fabergé pieces were nearly always privately commissioned. Miss Freudenstein says that her grandfather was a vastly rich man before the revolution – a porcelain manufacturer. Ninety-nine per cent of all Fabergé's output has found its way abroad. There are only a few pieces left in the Kremlin – described simply as "pre-revolutionary examples of Russian jewellery". The official Soviet view has always been that they are merely capitalist baubles. Officially they despise them as they officially despise their superb collection of French Impressionists.'

'So the Soviet still retain some examples of the work of this man Fabergé. Is it possible that this emerald affair could have lain secreted somewhere in the Kremlin through all these years?'

'Certainly. The Kremlin treasure is vast. No one knows what they keep hidden. They have only recently put on display what they have wanted to put on display.'

M drew on his pipe. His eyes through the smoke were bland, scarcely interested, 'So that, in theory, there is no reason why this emerald ball should not have been unearthed from the Kremlin, furnished with a faked history to establish ownership, and transferred abroad as a reward to some friend of Russia for services rendered?'

'None at all. It would be an ingenious method of greatly rewarding the beneficiary without the danger of paying large sums into his, or her, bank account.'

'But the final monetary reward would of course depend on the amount realized by the sale of the object – the auction price for instance?'

'Exactly.'

'And what do you expect this object to fetch at Sotheby's?'

'Impossible to say. Wartski's will certainly bid very high. But of course they wouldn't be prepared to tell anyone just how high – either on their own account for stock, so to speak, or acting on behalf of a customer. Much would depend on how high they are forced up by an underbidder. Anyway, not less than £100,000 I'd say.'

'Hm.' M's mouth turned down at the corners. 'Expensive hunk of jewellery.'

Dr Fanshawe was aghast at this bare-faced revelation of M's philistinism. He actually looked M straight in the face. 'My dear sir,' he expostulated, 'do you consider the stolen Goya, sold at Sotheby's for £140,000, that went to the National Gallery, just an expensive hunk, as you put it, of canvas and paint?'

M said placatingly, 'Forgive me, Dr Fanshawe. I expressed myself clumsily. I have never had the leisure to interest myself in works of art nor, on a naval officer's pay, the money to acquire any. I was just registering my dismay at the runaway prices being fetched at auction these days.'

'You are entitled to your views, sir,' said Dr Fanshawe stuffily.

Bond thought it was time to rescue M. He also wanted to get Dr Fanshawe out of the room so that they could get down to the professional aspects of this odd business. He got to his feet. He said to M, 'Well, sir, I don't think there is anything else I need to know. No doubt this will turn out to be perfectly straightforward (like hell it would!) and just a matter of one of your staff turning out to be a very lucky woman. But it's very kind of Dr Fanshawe to have gone to so much trouble.' He turned to Dr Fanshawe. 'Would you care to have a staff car to take you wherever you're going?'

'No thank you, thank you very much. It will be pleasant to walk across the park.'

Hands were shaken, goodbyes said and Bond showed the doctor out. Bond came back into the room. M had taken a bulky file, stamped with the top secret red star, out of a drawer and was already immersed in it. Bond took his seat again and waited. The room was silent save for the riffling of paper. This also stopped as M extracted a foolscap sheet of blue cardboard used for Confidential Staff Records and carefully read through the forest of close type on both sides.

Finally he slipped it back in the file and looked up.

'Yes,' he said and the blue eyes were bright with interest. 'It fits all right. The girl was born in Paris in 1935. Mother very active in the Resistance during the war. Helped run the Tulip Escape Route and got away with it. After the war, the girl went to the Sorbonne and then got a job in the Embassy, in the Naval Attaché's office, as an interpreter. You know the rest. She was compromised – some unattractive sexual business – by some of her mother's old Resistance friends who by then were working for the NKVD, and from then on she has been working under Control. She applied, no doubt on instruction, for British citizenship. Her clearance from the Embassy and her mother's Resistance record helped her to get that by 1959, and she was then recommended to us by the FO. But it was there that she made her big mistake. She asked for a year's leave before coming to us and was next reported by the Hutchinson network in the Leningrad espionage school. There she presumably received the usual training and we had to decide what to do about her. Section 100 thought up the Purple Cipher operation and you know the rest. She's been working for three years inside headquarters for the KGB and now she's getting her reward – this emerald ball thing worth £100,000. And that's interesting on two counts. First it means that the KGB is totally hooked on the Purple Cipher or they wouldn't be making this fantastic payment. That's good news. It means that we can hot up the material we're passing over – put across some Grade 3 deception material and perhaps even move up to Grade 2. Secondly, it explains something we've never been able to understand – that this girl hasn't hitherto received a single payment for her services. We were worried by that. She had an account at Glyn, Mills that only registered her monthly pay cheque of around £50. And she's consistently lived within it. Now she's getting her pay-off in one large lump sum via this bauble we've been learning about. All very satisfactory.'

M reached for the ashtray made out of a twelve-inch shell base and rapped out his pipe with the air of a man who has done a good afternoon's work.

Bond shifted in his chair. He badly needed a cigarette, but he wouldn't have dreamed of lighting one. He wanted one to help him focus his thoughts. He felt that there were some ragged edges to this problem – one particularly. He said, mildly, 'Have we ever caught up with her local Control, sir? How does she get her instructions?'

'Doesn't need to,' said M impatiently, busying himself with his pipe. 'Once she'd got hold of the Purple Cipher all she needed to do was hold down her job. Damn it man, she's pouring the stuff into their lap six times a day. What sort of instructions would they need to give her? I doubt if the KGB men in London even know of her existence – perhaps the Resident Director does, but as you know we don't even know who he is. Give my eyes to find out.'

Bond suddenly had a flash of intuition. It was as if a

camera had started grinding in his skull, grinding out a length of clear film. He said quietly, 'It might be that this business at Sotheby's could show him to us – show us who he is.'

'What the devil are you talking about, 007? Explain yourself.'

'Well, sir,' Bond's voice was calm with certainty, 'you remember what this Dr Fanshawe said about an underbidder – someone to make these Wartski merchants go to their very top price. If the Russians don't seem to know or care very much about Fabergé, as Dr Fanshawe says, they may have no very clear idea what this thing's really worth. The KGB wouldn't be likely to know about such things anyway. They may imagine it's only worth its break-up value – say ten or twenty thousand pounds for the emerald. That sort of sum would make more sense than the small fortune the girl's going to get if Dr Fanshawe's right. Well, if the Resident Director is the only man who knows about this girl, he will be the only man who knows she's been paid. So he'll be the underbidder. He'll be sent to Sotheby's and told to push the sale through the roof. I'm certain of it. So we'll be able to identify him and we'll have enough on him to have him sent home. He just won't know what's hit him. Nor will the KGB. If I can go to the sale and bowl him out and we've got the place covered with cameras, and the auction records, we can get the FO to declare him persona non grata inside a week. And Resident Directors don't grow on trees. It may be months before the KGB can appoint a replacement.'

M said, thoughtfully, 'Perhaps you've got something there.' He swivelled his chair round and gazed out of the big window towards the jagged skyline of London. Finally he said, over his shoulder, 'All right, 007. Go and see the Chief of Staff and set the machinery up. I'll square things with Five. It's their territory, but it's our bird. There won't be any trouble. But don't go and get carried away and bid for this bit of rubbish yourself. I haven't got the money to spare.'

Bond said, 'No, sir.' He got to his feet and went quickly out of the room. He thought he had been very clever and he wanted to see if he had. He didn't want M to change his mind.

Wartski has a modest, ultra-modern frontage at 138 Regent Street. The window, with a restrained show of modern and antique jewellery, gave no hint that these were the greatest Fabergé-dealers in the world. The interior – grey carpet, walls panelled in sycamore, a few unpretentious vitrines – held none of the excitement of Cartier's, Boucheron or Van Cleef, but the group of framed Royal Warrants from Queen Mary, the Queen Mother, the Queen, King Paul of Greece and the unlikely King Frederick IX of Denmark, suggested that this was no ordinary jeweller.

James Bond asked for Mr Kenneth Snowman. A good-looking, very well-dressed man of about forty rose from a group of men sitting with their heads together at the back of the room and came forward.

Bond said quietly, 'I'm from the CID. Can we have a talk? Perhaps you'd like to check my credentials first. My name's James Bond. But you'll have to go direct to Sir Ronald Vallance or his P.A. I'm not directly on the strength at Scotland Yard. Sort of liaison job.'

The intelligent, observant eyes didn't appear even to look him over. The man smiled. 'Come on downstairs. Just having a talk with some American friends – sort of correspondents really. From "Old Russia" on Fifth Avenue.'

'I know the place,' said Bond. 'Full of rich-looking icons and so on. Not far from the Pierre.'

'That's right.' Mr Snowman seemed even more reassured. He led the way down a narrow, thickly carpeted stairway into a large and glittering show-room which was obviously the real treasure house of the shop. Gold and diamonds and cut stones winked from lit cases round the walls.

'Have a seat. Cigarette?'

Bond took one of his own. 'It's about this Fabergé piece that's coming up at Sotheby's tomorrow – this Emerald Sphere.'

'Ah, yes.' Mr Snowman's clear brow furrowed anxiously. 'No trouble about it I hope?'

'Not from your point of view. But we're very

interested in the actual sale. We know about the owner, Miss Freudenstein. We think there may be an attempt to raise the bidding artificially. We're interested in the underbidder – assuming, that is, that your firm will be leading the field, so to speak.'

'Well, er, yes,' said Mr Snowman with rather careful candour. 'We're certainly going to go after it. But it'll sell for a huge price. Between you and me, we believe the V and A are going to bid, and probably the Metropolitan. But is it some crook you're after? If so you needn't worry. This is out of their class.'

Bond said, 'No. We're not looking for a crook.' He wondered how far to go with this man. Because people are very careful with the secrets of their own business doesn't mean that they'll be careful with the secrets of yours. Bond picked up a wood and ivory plaque that lay on the table. It said:

> It is naught, it is naught, saith the buyer.
> But when he is gone his way, he boasteth.
> – Proverbs XX, 14

Bond was amused. He said so. 'You can read the whole history of the bazaar, of the dealer and the customer, behind that quotation,' he said. He looked Mr Snowman straight in the eyes. 'I need that sort of nose, that sort of intuition in this case. Will you give me a hand?'

'Certainly. If you'll tell me how I can help.' He waved a hand. 'If it's secrets you're worried about, please don't worry. Jewellers are used to them.

Scotland Yard will probably give my firm a clean bill in that respect. Heaven knows we've had enough to do with them over the years.'

'And if I told you that I'm from the Ministry of Defence?'

'Same thing,' said Mr Snowman. 'You can naturally rely absolutely on my discretion!'

Bond made up his mind. 'All right. Well, all this comes under the Official Secrets Act, of course. We suspect that the underbidder, presumably to you, will be a Soviet Agent. My job is to establish his identity. Can't tell you any more, I'm afraid. And you don't actually need to know any more. All I want is to go with you to Sotheby's tomorrow night and for you to help me spot the man. No medals, I'm afraid, but we'd be extremely grateful.'

Mr Kenneth Snowman's eyes glinted with enthusiasm. 'Of course. Delighted to help in any way. But,' he looked doubtful, 'you know it's not necessarily going to be all that easy. Peter Wilson, the head of Sotheby's, who'll be taking the sale, would be the only person who could tell us for sure – that is, if the bidder wants to stay secret. There are dozens of ways of bidding without making any movement at all. But if the bidder fixes his method, his code so to speak, with Peter Wilson before the sale, Peter wouldn't think of letting anyone in on the code. It would give the bidder's game away to reveal his limit. And that's a close secret, as you can imagine, in the rooms. And a thousand times not if you come

with me. I shall probably be setting the pace. I
already know how far I'm going to go – for a client
by the way – but it would make my job vastly easier
if I could tell how far the underbidder's going to go.
As it is, what you've told me has been a great help.
I shall warn my man to put his sights even higher. If
this chap of yours has got a strong nerve, he may
push me very hard indeed. And there will be others in
the field of course. It sounds as if this is going to be
quite a night. They're putting it on television and
asking all the millionaires and dukes and duchesses
for the sort of gala performance Sotheby's do rather
well. Wonderful publicity of course. By jove, if they
knew there was cloak-and-dagger stuff mixed up
with the sale, there'd be a riot! Now then, is there anything else to go into? Just spot this man and that's
all?'

'That's all. How much do you think this thing will
go for?'

Mr Snowman tapped his teeth with a gold pencil.
'Well now, you see that's where I have to keep quiet.
I know how high I'm going to go, but that's my
client's secret.' He paused and looked thoughtful,
'Let's say that if it goes for less than £100,000 we'll
be surprised.'

'I see,' said Bond. 'Now then, how do I get into
the sale?'

Mr Snowman produced an elegant alligator-skin
notecase and extracted two engraved bits of paste-
board. He handed one over. 'That's my wife's. I'll

get her one somewhere else in the rooms. B5 – well placed in the centre front. I'm B6.'

Bond took the ticket. It said:

Sotheby & Co.

Sale of

A Casket of Magnificent Jewels
and
A Unique Object of Vertu by Carl Fabergé

The Property of a Lady
Admit one to the Main Sale Room
Tuesday, 20 June, at 9.30 pm precisely

ENTRANCE IN ST GEORGE STREET

'It's not the old Georgian entrance in Bond Street,' commented Mr Snowman. 'They have an awning and red carpet out from their back door now that Bond Street's one-way. Now,' he got up from his chair, 'would you care to see some Fabergé? We've got some pieces here my father bought from the Kremlin around 1927. It'll give you some idea what all the fuss is about, though of course the Emerald Sphere's incomparably finer than anything I can show you by Fabergé apart from the Imperial Easter Eggs.'

Later, dazzled by the diamonds, the multi-coloured gold, the silken sheen of translucent enamels, James Bond walked up and out of the Aladdin's Cave under

Regent Street and went off to spend the rest of the day in drab offices around Whitehall planning drearily minute arrangements for the identification and photographing of a man in a crowded room who did not yet possess a face or an identity but who was certainly the top Soviet spy in London.

Through the next day, Bond's excitement mounted. He found an excuse to go into the Communications Section and wander into the little room where Miss Maria Freudenstein and two assistants were working the cipher machines that handled the Purple Cipher dispatches. He picked up an *en clair* file – he had freedom of access to most material at headquarters – and ran his eye down the carefully edited paragraphs that, in half an hour or so, would be spiked, unread, by some Junior CIA clerk in Washington and, in Moscow, be handed, with reverence, to a topranking officer of the KGB. He joked with the two junior girls, but Maria Freudenstein only looked up from her machine to give him a polite smile and Bond's skin crawled minutely at this proximity to treachery and at the black and deadly secret locked up beneath the frilly white blouse. She was an unattractive girl with a pale, rather pimply skin, black hair and a vaguely unwashed appearance. Such a girl would be unloved, make few friends, have chips on her shoulder – more particularly in view of her illegitimacy – and a grouse against society. Perhaps her only pleasure in life was the triumphant secret she harboured in that flattish bosom – the knowledge that she was cleverer than all those around her, that she was, every day, hitting back against the world – the world that despised, or just ignored her, because of her plainness – with all her might. One day they'd be sorry! It was a common neurotic pattern – the revenge of the ugly duckling on society.

Bond wandered off down the corridor to his own office. By tonight that girl would have made a fortune, been paid her thirty pieces of silver a thousandfold. Perhaps the money would change her character, bring her happiness. She would be able to afford the best beauty specialists, the best clothes, a pretty flat. But M had said he was now going to hot up the Purple Cipher Operation, try a more dangerous level of deception. This would be dicey work. One false step, one incautious lie, an ascertainable falsehood in a message, and KGB would smell a rat. One more, and they would know they were being hoaxed and probably had been ignominiously hoaxed for three years. Such a shameful revelation would bring quick revenge. It would be assumed that Maria Freudenstein had been acting as a double agent, working for the British as well as the Russians. She would inevitably and quickly be liquidated – perhaps with a cyanide pistol Bond had been reading about only the day before.

James Bond, looking out of the window across the trees in Regent's Park, shrugged. Thank God it was

none of his business. The girl's fate wasn't in his
hands. She was caught in the grimy machine of
espionage and she would be lucky if she lived to
spend a tenth of the fortune she was going to gain in
a few hours in the auction rooms.

There was a line of cars and taxis blocking George
Street behind Sotheby's. Bond paid off his taxi and
joined the crowd filtering under the awning and up
the steps. He was handed a catalogue by the uni-
formed commissionaire who inspected his ticket, and
went up the broad stairs with the fashionable, excited
crowd and along a gallery and into the main auction
room that was already thronged. He found his seat
next to Mr Snowman, who was writing figures on a
pad on his knee, and looked round him.

The lofty room was perhaps as large as a tennis
court. It had the look and the smell of age and the
two large chandeliers, to fit in with the period, blazed
warmly in contrast to the strip lighting along the
vaulted ceiling whose glass roof was partly obscured
by a blind, still half-drawn against the sun that would
have been blazing down on the afternoon's sale.
Miscellaneous pictures and tapestries hung on the
olive green walls and batteries of television and other
cameras (amongst them the MI5 cameraman with a
press pass from the *Sunday Times*) were clustered with
their handlers on a platform built out from the middle
of a giant tapestried hunting scene. There were

perhaps a hundred dealers and spectators sitting attentively on small gilt chairs. All eyes were focused on the slim, good-looking auctioneer talking quietly from the raised wooden pulpit. He was dressed in an immaculate dinner jacket with a red carnation in the buttonhole. He spoke unemphatically and without gestures.

'Fifteen thousand pounds. And sixteen,' a pause. A glance at someone in the front row. 'Against you, sir.' The flick of a catalogue being raised. 'Seventeen thousand pounds I am bid. Eighteen. Nineteen. I am bid twenty thousand pounds.' And so the quiet voice went, calmly, unhurriedly on while down among the audience the equally impassive bidders signalled their responses to the litany.

'What is he selling?' asked Bond, opening his catalogue.

'Lot 40,' said Mr Snowman. 'That diamond rivière the porter's holding on the black velvet tray. It'll probably go for about twenty-five. An Italian is bidding against a couple of Frenchmen. Otherwise they'd have got it for twenty. I only went to fifteen. Liked to have got it. Wonderful stones. But there it is.'

Sure enough, the price stuck at twenty-five thousand and the hammer, held by its head and not by its handle, came down with soft authority. 'Yours, sir,' said Mr Peter Wilson and a sales clerk hurried down the aisle to confirm the identity of the bidder.

'I'm disappointed,' said Bond.

Mr Snowman looked up from his catalogue, 'Why is that?'

'I've never been to an auction before and I always thought the auctioneer banged his gavel three times and said going, going, gone, so as to give the bidders a last chance.'

Mr Snowman laughed. 'You might still find that operating in the Shires or in Ireland, but it hasn't been the fashion at London sale rooms since I've been attending them.'

'Pity. It adds to the drama.'

'You'll get plenty of that in a minute. This is the last lot before the curtain goes up.'

One of the porters had reverently uncoiled a glittering mass of rubies and diamonds on his black velvet tray. Bond looked at the catalogue. It said 'Lot 41' which the luscious prose described as:

A PAIR OF FINE AND IMPORTANT RUBY AND DIAMOND BRACELETS, the front of each in the form of an elliptical cluster composed of one larger and two smaller rubies within a border of cushion-shaped diamonds, the sides and back formed of simpler clusters alternating with diamond openwork scroll motifs springing from single-stone ruby centres millegriffe-set in gold, running between chains of rubies and diamonds linked alternately, the clasp also in the form of an elliptical cluster.

★ According to family tradition, this lot was formerly the property of Mrs Fitzherbert (1756–1837) whose marriage to the Prince of Wales afterwards Geo. IV was definitely established when in 1905 a sealed packet deposited at Coutts Bank in 1833 and opened by Royal permission disclosed the marriage certificate and other conclusive proofs.

These bracelets were probably given by Mrs Fitzherbert to her niece, who was described by the Duke of Orleans as 'the prettiest girl in England'.

While the bidding progressed, Bond slipped out of his seat and went down the aisle to the back of the room where the overflow audience spread out into the New Gallery and the Entrance Hall to watch the sale on closed circuit television. He casually inspected the crowd, seeking any face he could recognize from the 200 members of the Soviet embassy staff whose photographs, clandestinely obtained, he had been studying during the past days. But amidst an audience that defied classification – a mixture of dealers, amateur collectors and what could be broadly classified as rich pleasure-seekers – was not a feature, let alone a face, that he could recognize except from the gossip columns. One or two sallow faces might have been Russian, but equally they might have belonged to half a dozen European races. There was a scattering of dark glasses, but dark glasses are no longer a disguise. Bond went back to his seat. Presumably the man would have to divulge himself when the bidding began.

'Fourteen thousand I am bid. And fifteen. Fifteen thousand.' The hammer came down. 'Yours, sir.'

There was a hum of excitement and a fluttering of catalogues. Mr Snowman wiped his forehead with a white silk handkerchief. He turned to Bond, 'Now I'm afraid you are more or less on your own. I've got to pay attention to the bidding and anyway for some unknown reason it's considered bad form to look over one's shoulder to see who's bidding against you – if you're in the trade that's to say – so I'll only be able to spot him if he's somewhere up front here, and I'm afraid that's unlikely. Pretty well all dealers, but you can stare around as much as you like. What you've got to do is to watch Peter Wilson's eyes and then try and see who he's looking at, or who's looking at him. If you can spot the man, which may be quite difficult, note any movement he makes, even the very smallest. Whatever the man does – scratching his head, pulling at the lobe of his ear or whatever, will be a code he's arranged with Peter Wilson. I'm afraid he won't do anything obvious like raising his catalogue. Do you get me? And don't forget that he may make absolutely no movement at all until right at the end when he's pushed me as far as he thinks I'll go, then he'll want to sign off. Mark you,' Mr Snowman smiled, 'when we get to the last lap I'll put plenty of heat on him and try and make him show his hand. That's assuming of course that we are the only two bidders left in.' He looked enigmatic. 'And I think you can take it that we shall be.'

From the man's certainty, James Bond felt pretty sure that Mr Snowman had been given instructions to get the Emerald Sphere at any cost.

A sudden hush fell as a tall pedestal draped in black

velvet was brought in with ceremony and positioned in front of the auctioneer's rostrum. Then a handsome oval case of what looked like white velvet was placed on top of the pedestal and, with reverence, an elderly porter in grey uniform with wine red sleeves, collar and back belt, unlocked it and lifted out Lot 42, placed it on the black velvet and removed the case. The cricket ball of polished emerald on its exquisite base glowed with a supernatural green fire and the jewels on its surface and on the opalescent meridian winked their various colours. There was a gasp of admiration from the audience and even the clerks and experts behind the rostrum and sitting at the tall counting-house desk beside the auctioneer, accustomed to the Crown jewels of Europe parading before their eyes, leaned forward to get a better look.

James Bond turned to his catalogue. There it was, in heavy type and in prose as stickily luscious as a butterscotch sundae:

THE TERRESTRIAL GLOBE
DESIGNED IN 1917 BY CARL FABERGÉ FOR
A RUSSIAN GENTLEMAN AND NOW THE
PROPERTY OF HIS GRANDDAUGHTER
42 A VERY IMPORTANT FABERGÉ TERRESTRIAL
GLOBE.

A sphere carved from an extraordinarily large piece of Siberian emerald matrix weighing approximately one thousand three hundred carats and of a superb colour and vivid translucence, represents a terrestrial globe supported upon an elaborate *rocaille* scroll mount finely chased in *quatre-couleur* gold and set with a profusion of rose-diamonds and small emeralds of intense colour, to form a table-clock.

Around this mount six gold *putti* disport themselves among cloud-forms which are naturalistically rendered in carved rock-crystal finished matt and veined with fine lines of tiny rose-diamonds.

The Globe itself, the surface of which is meticulously engraved with a map of the world with the principal cities indicated by brilliant diamonds embedded within gold collets, rotates mechanically on an axis controlled by a small clock-movement, by *G. Moser*, signed, which is concealed in the base, and is girdled by a fixed gold belt enamelled opalescent oyster along a reserved path in *champlevé* technique over a moiré *guillochage* with painted Roman numerals in pale sepia enamel serving as the dial of the clock, and a single triangular pigeon-blood Burma ruby of about five carats set into the surface of the orb, pointing the hour.

Height: 7½ in. *Workmaster, Henrik Wigström*. In the original double-opening white velvet, satin-lined, oviform case with the gold key fitted in the base.

★ The theme of this magnificent sphere is one that had inspired Fabergé some fifteen years earlier, as evidenced in the miniature terrestrial globe which forms part of the Royal Collection at Sandringham. (See plate 280 in *The Art of Carl Fabergé*, by A. Kenneth Snowman.)

After a brief and searching glance round the room, Mr Wilson banged his hammer softly. 'Lot 42 – an object of vertu by Carl Fabergé.' A pause. 'Twenty thousand pounds I am bid.'

Mr Snowman whispered to Bond, 'That means he's

probably got a bid of at least fifty. This is simply to get things moving.'

Catalogues fluttered. 'And thirty, forty, fifty thousand pounds I am bid. And sixty, seventy, and eighty thousand pounds. And ninety.' A pause and then: 'One hundred thousand pounds I am bid.'

There was a rattle of applause round the room. The cameras had swivelled to a youngish man, one of three on a raised platform to the left of the auctioneer who were speaking softly into telephones. Mr Snowman commented, 'That's one of Sotheby's young men. He'll be on an open line to America. I should think that's the Metropolitan bidding, but it might be anybody. Now it's time for me to get to work.' Mr Snowman flicked up his rolled catalogue.

'And ten,' said the auctioneer. The man spoke into his telephone and nodded. 'And twenty.'

Again a flick from Mr Snowman.

'And thirty.'

The man on the telephone seemed to be speaking rather more words than before into his mouthpiece – perhaps giving his estimate of how much further the price was likely to go. He gave a slight shake of his head in the direction of the auctioneer and Peter Wilson looked away from him and round the room.

'One hundred and thirty thousand pounds I am bid,' he repeated quietly.

Mr Snowman said, softly, to Bond, 'Now you'd better watch out. America seems to have signed off. It's time for your man to start pushing me.'

James Bond slid out of his place and went and stood amongst a group of reporters in a corner to the left of the rostrum. Peter Wilson's eyes were directed towards the far right hand corner of the room. Bond could detect no movement, but the auctioneer announced, 'And forty thousand pounds.' He looked down at Mr Snowman. After a long pause Mr Snowman raised five fingers. Bond guessed that this was part of his process of putting the heat on. He was showing reluctance, hinting that he was near the end of his tether.

'One hundred and forty-five thousand.' Again the piercing glance towards the back of the room. Again no movement. But again some signal had been exchanged. 'One hundred and fifty thousand pounds.'

There was a buzz of comment and some desultory clapping. This time Mr Snowman's reaction was even slower and the auctioneer twice repeated the last bid. Finally he looked directly at Mr Snowman. 'Against you, sir.' At last Mr Snowman raised five fingers.

'One hundred and fifty-five thousand pounds.'

James Bond was beginning to sweat. He had got absolutely nowhere and the bidding must surely be coming to an end. The auctioneer repeated the bid.

And now there was the tiniest movement. At the back of the room, a chunky-looking man in a dark suit reached up and unobtrusively took off his dark glasses. It was a smooth, nondescript face – the sort of face that might belong to a bank manager, a member of Lloyd's, or a doctor. This must have been the prearranged code with the auctioneer. So long as the man wore his dark glasses he would raise in tens of thousands. When he took them off, he had quit.

Bond shot a quick glance towards the bank of cameramen. Yes, the MI5 photographer was on his toes. He had also seen the movement. He lifted his camera deliberately and there was the quick glare of a flash. Bond got back to his seat and whispered to Snowman, 'Got him. Be in touch with you tomorrow. Thanks a lot.' Mr Snowman only nodded. His eyes remained glued on the auctioneer.

Bond slipped out of his place and walked swiftly down the aisle as the auctioneer said for the third time, 'One hundred and fifty-five thousand pounds I am bid,' and then softly brought down his hammer. 'Yours, sir.'

Bond got to the back of the room before the audience had risen, applauding, to its feet. His quarry was hemmed in amongst the gilt chairs. He had now put on his dark glasses again and Bond put on a pair of his own. He contrived to slip into the crowd and get behind the man as the chattering crowd streamed down the stairs. The hair grew low down on the back of the man's rather squat neck and the lobes of his ears were pinched in close to his head. He had a slight hump, perhaps only a bone deformation, high up on his back. Bond suddenly remembered.

This was Piotr Malinowski, with the official title on the Embassy staff of 'Agricultural Attaché'. So!

Outside, the man began walking swiftly towards Conduit Street. James Bond got unhurriedly into a taxi with its engine running and its flag down. He said to the driver, 'That's him. Take it easy.'

'Yes, sir,' said the MI5 driver, pulling away from the curb.

The man picked up a taxi in Bond Street. The tail in the mixed evening traffic was easy. Bond's satisfaction mounted as the Russian's taxi turned up north of the Park and along Bayswater. It was just a question whether he would turn down the private entrance into Kensington Palace Gardens, where the first mansion on the left is the massive building of the Soviet Embassy. If he did, that would clinch matters. The two patrolling policemen, the usual Embassy guards, had been specially picked that night. It was their job just to confirm that the occupant of the leading taxi actually entered the Soviet Embassy.

Then, with the Secret Service evidence and the evidence of Bond and of the MI5 cameraman, there would be enough for the Foreign Office to declare Comrade Piotr Malinowski persona non grata on the grounds of espionage activity and send him packing. In the grim chess game that is secret service work, the Russians would have lost a queen. It would have been a very satisfactory visit to the auction rooms.

The leading taxi *did* turn in through the big iron gates.

Bond smiled with grim satisfaction. He leant forward.

'Thanks, driver. Headquarters please.'

The Living Daylights

JAMES BOND LAY at the five-hundred-yard firing point of the famous Century Range at Bisley. The white peg in the grass beside him said 4.4 and the same number was repeated high up on the distant butt above the single six-foot-square target that, to the human eye and in the late summer dusk, looked no larger than a postage stamp. But Bond's lens, an infra-red Sniperscope fixed above his rifle, covered the whole canvas. He could even clearly distinguish the pale-blue and beige colours into which the target was divided, and the six-inch semicircular bull looked as big as the half moon that was already beginning to show low down in the darkening sky above the distant crest of Chobham Ridges.

James Bond's last shot had been an inner left – not good enough. He took another glance at the yellow-and-blue wind flags. They were streaming across range from the east rather more stiffly than when he had begun his shoot half an hour before, and he set two clicks more to the right on the wind gauge and traversed the cross-wires on the Sniperscope back to the point of aim. Then he settled himself, put his trigger finger gently inside the guard and on to the curve of the trigger, shallowed his breathing and very, very softly squeezed.

The vicious crack of the shot boomed across the empty range. The target disappeared below ground and at once the 'dummy' came up in its place. Yes, the black panel was in the bottom right-hand corner this time, not in the bottom left: a bull.

'Good,' said the voice of the Chief Range Officer from behind and above him. 'Stay with it.'

The target was already up again and Bond put his cheek back to its warm patch on the chunky wooden stock and his eye to the rubber eyepiece of the 'scope. He wiped his gun hand down the side of his trousers and took the pistol grip that jutted sharply down below the trigger guard. He splayed his legs an inch more. Now there were to be five rounds rapid. It would be interesting to see if that would produce 'fade'. He guessed not. This extraordinary weapon the Armourer had somehow got his hands on gave one the feeling that a standing man at a mile would be easy meat. It was mostly a ·308 calibre International Experimental Target rifle built by Winchester to help American marksmen at World Championships, and it had the usual gadgets of super-accurate target weapons – a curled aluminium 'hand' at the back of the butt that extended under the armpit and held the stock firmly into the shoulder, and an adjustable pinion below the rifle's centre of gravity to allow the stock to be 'nailed' into its grooved wooden rest. The Armourer had had the usual single-shot bolt action replaced by a five-shot magazine, and he had assured Bond that if he would allow only two seconds between shots to steady the weapon there would be no fade even at five hundred yards. For the job that

Bond had to do, he guessed that two seconds might be a dangerous loss of time if he missed with his first shot. Anyway, M had said that the range would be not more than three hundred yards. Bond would cut it down to one second – almost continuous fire.

'Ready?'

'Yes.'

'I'll give you a count-down from five. Now! Five, four, three, two, one. Fire!'

The ground shuddered slightly and the air sang as the five whirling scraps of cupro-nickel spat off into the dusk. The target went down and quickly rose again decorated with four small white discs closely grouped on the bull. There was no fifth disc – not even a black one to show an inner or an outer.

'The last round was low,' said the Range Officer lowering his night-glasses. 'Thanks for the contribution. We sift the sand on those butts at the end of every year. Never get less than fifteen tons of good lead and copper scrap out of them. Good money.'

Bond had got to his feet. Corporal Menzies from the Armourers' section appeared from the pavilion of the Gun Club and knelt down to dismantle the Winchester and its rest. He looked up at Bond. He said with a hint of criticism, 'You were taking it a bit fast, sir. Last round was bound to jump wide.'

'I know, Corporal. I wanted to see how fast I *could* take it. I'm not blaming the weapon. It's the hell of a fine job. Please tell the Armourer so from me. Now I'd better get moving. You're finding your own way back to London, aren't you?'

'Yes. Good night, sir.'

The Chief Range Officer handed Bond a record of his shoot – two sighting shots and then ten rounds at each hundred yards up to five hundred. 'Damned good firing with this visibility. You ought to come back next year and have a bash at the Queen's Prize. It's open to all comers nowadays – British Common-wealth, that is.'

'Thanks. Trouble is, I'm not all that much in England. And thanks for spotting for me.' Bond glanced at the distant Clock Tower. On either side, the red danger flag and the red signal drum were coming down to show that firing had ceased. The hands stood at nine fifteen. 'I'd like to have bought you a drink, but I've got an appointment in London. Can we hold it over until that Queen's Prize you were talking about?'

The Range Officer nodded noncommittally. He had been looking forward to finding out more about this man who had appeared out of the blue after a flurry of signals from the Ministry of Defence and had then proceeded to score well over ninety per cent at all distances, and that after the range was closed for the night and visibility was poor to bad. And why had he, who only officiated at the annual July meeting, been ordered to be present? And why had he been told to see that Bond had a six-inch bull at 500 instead of the regulation fifteen-inch? And why this flummery with the danger flag and signal drum that were only used on ceremonial occasions? To put pressure on the man? To give an edge of urgency to the shoot? Bond. Commander James Bond. The NRA would surely have a record of anyone who could shoot like that. He'd remember to give them a call. Funny time to have an appointment in London. Probably a girl. The Range Officer's undistinguished face assumed a disgruntled expression. Sort of fellow who got all the girls he wanted.

The two men walked through the handsome façade of Club Row behind the range to Bond's car that stood opposite the bullet-pitted iron reproduction of Landseer's famous 'Running Deer'. 'Nice-looking job,' commented the Range Officer. 'Never seen a body like that on a Continental. Have it made specially?'

'Yes. The Sports Saloons are really only two-seaters. And damned little luggage space. So I got Mulliner's to make it into a real two-seater with plenty of boot. Selfish car, I'm afraid. Well, good night. And thanks again.' The exhaust boomed healthily and the back wheels briefly spat gravel.

The Chief Range Officer watched the ruby lights vanish up King's Avenue towards the London road. He turned on his heel and went to find Corporal Menzies on a search for information that was to prove fruitless. The corporal remained as wooden as the big mahogany box he was in the process of loading into a khaki Land-Rover without military symbols. The Range Officer was a major. He tried pulling his rank without success. The Land-Rover hammered away in Bond's wake. The major walked moodily off to the offices of the National Rifle Association to try and find out what he wanted in the library under 'Bond, J.'.

James Bond's appointment was not with a girl. It was with a BEA flight to Hanover and Berlin. As he bit off the miles to London Airport, pushing the big car hard so as to have plenty of time for a drink, three drinks, before the take-off, only part of his mind was on the road. The rest was re-examining, for the umpteenth time, the sequence that was now leading him to an appointment with an aeroplane. But only an interim appointment. His final rendezvous on one of the next three nights in Berlin was with a man. He had to see this man and infallibly shoot him dead.

When, at around two thirty that afternoon, James Bond had gone in through the double-padded doors and had sat down opposite the turned-away profile on the other side of the big desk, he had sensed trouble. There was no greeting. M's head was sunk into his stiff turned-down collar in a Churchillian pose of gloomy reflection, and there was a droop of bitterness at the corners of his lips. He swivelled his chair round to face Bond, gave him an appraising glance as if, Bond thought, to see that his tie was straight and his hair properly brushed, and then began speaking, fast, clipping off his sentences as if he wanted to be rid of what he was saying, and of Bond, as quickly as possible.

'Number 272. He's a good man. You won't have come across him. Simple reason that he's been holed up in Novaya Zemlya since the war. Now he's trying to get out – loaded with stuff. Atomic and rockets. And their plan for a whole new series of tests. For 1961. To put the heat on the West. Something to do with Berlin. Don't quite get the picture but the FO say if it's true it's terrific. Makes nonsense of the Geneva Conference and all this blether about nuclear disarmament the Communist bloc are putting out. He's got as far as East Berlin. But he's got practically the whole of the KGB on his tail – and the East German security forces of course. He's holed up somewhere in the city and he got one message over to us – that he'd be coming across between six and seven pm on one of the next three nights – tomorrow, next day, or the day after. He gave the crossing point. Trouble is,' the downward curve of M's lips became even more bitter, 'the courier he used was a double. Station WB bowled him out yesterday. Quite by chance. Had a lucky break with one of the KGB codes. The courier'll be flown out for trial, of course. But that won't help. The KGB know that 272 will be making a run for it. They know when. They know where. They know just as much as we do and no more. Now, the code we

cracked was a one-day-only setting on their machines.
But we got the whole of that day's traffic and that
was good enough. They plan to shoot him on the
run. At this street crossing between East and West
Berlin he gave us in his message. They're mounting
quite an operation – operation "Extase" they call it.
Put their best sniper on the job. All we know about
him is that his code name is the Russian for "Trigger". Station WB guess he's the same man they've
used before for sniper work. Long-range stuff across
the frontier. He's going to be guarding this crossing
every night and his job is to get 272. Of course
they'd obviously prefer to do a smoother job with
machine-guns and what have you. But it's quiet in
Berlin at the moment and apparently the word is it's
got to stay so. Anyway,' M shrugged, 'they've got
confidence in this "Trigger" operator and that's the
way it's going to be!'

'Where do I come in, sir?' James Bond had guessed
the answer, guessed why M was showing his dislike
of the whole business. This was going to be dirty
work and Bond, because he belonged to the Double-
O Section, had been chosen for it. Perversely, Bond
wanted to force M to put it in black and white. This
was going to be bad news, dirty news, and he didn't
want to hear it from one of the Section officers, or
even from the Chief of Staff. This was to be murder.
All right. Let M bloody well say so.

'Where do you come in, 007?' M looked coldly
across the desk. 'You know where you come in.

You've got to kill this sniper. And you've got to kill him before he gets 272. That's all. Is that understood?' The clear blue eyes remained cold as ice. But Bond knew that they remained so only with an effort of will. M didn't like sending any man to a killing. But, when it had to be done, he always put on this fierce, cold act of command. Bond knew why. It was to take some of the pressure, some of the guilt, off the killer's shoulders.

So now Bond, who knew these things, decided to make it easy and quick for M. He got to his feet. 'That's all right, sir. I suppose the Chief of Staff has got all the gen. I'd better go and put in some practice. It wouldn't do to miss.' He walked to the door.

M said quietly, 'Sorry to have to hand this to you. Nasty job. But it's got to be done well.'

'I'll do my best, sir.' James Bond walked out and closed the door behind him. He didn't like the job, but on the whole he'd rather have it himself than have the responsibility of ordering someone else to go and do it.

The Chief of Staff had been only a shade more sympathetic. 'Sorry you've bought this one, James,' he had said. 'But Tanqueray was definite that he hadn't got anyone good enough on his Station, and this isn't the sort of job you can ask a regular soldier to do. Plenty of top marksmen in the BAOR, but a live target needs another kind of nerve. Anyway, I've been on to Bisley and fixed a shoot for you tonight at eight fifteen when the ranges will be closed. Visibility should be about the same as you'll be getting in Berlin around an hour earlier. The Armourer's got the gun – a real target job, and he's sending it down with one of his men. You'll find your own way. Then you're booked on a midnight BEA charter flight to Berlin. Take a taxi to this address.' He handed Bond a piece of paper. 'Go up to the fourth floor and you'll find Tanqueray's Number 2 waiting for you. Then I'm afraid you'll just have to sit it out for the next three days.'

'How about the gun? Am I supposed to take it through the German customs in a golf bag or something?'

The Chief of Staff hadn't been amused. 'It'll go over in the FO bag. You'll have it by tomorrow midday.' He had reached for a signal pad. 'Well, you'd better get cracking. I'll just let Tanqueray know everything's fixed.'

James Bond glanced down at the dim blue face of the dashboard clock. Ten fifteen. With any luck by this time tomorrow it would all be finished. After all, it was the life of this man 'Trigger' against the life of 272. It wasn't *exactly* murder. Pretty near it, though. He gave a vicious blast on his triple windhorns at an inoffensive family saloon, took the roundabout in a quite unnecessary dry skid, wrenched the wheel harshly to correct it and pointed the nose of the

Bentley towards the distant glow that was London
Airport.

The ugly six-storey building at the corner of Koch-
strasse and the Wilhelmstrasse was the only one
standing in a waste of empty bombed space. Bond
paid off his taxi and got a brief impression of waist-
high weeds and half-tidied rubble walls stretching
away to a big deserted crossroads lit by a central
cluster of yellowish arc lamps, before he pushed the
bell for the fourth floor and at once heard the click of
the door-opener. The door closed itself behind him
and he walked over the uncarpeted cement floor to
the old-fashioned lift. The smell of cabbage, cheap
cigar smoke and stale sweat reminded him of other
apartment houses in Germany and Central Europe.
Even the sigh and faint squeal of the slow lift were
part of a hundred assignments when he had been
fired off by M, like a projectile, at some distant target
where a problem waited for his coming, waited to be
solved by him. At least this time the reception committee was on his side. This time there was nothing
to fear at the top of the stairs.

Number 2 of Secret Service Station WB was a
lean, tense man in his early forties. He wore the uniform of his profession – well-cut, well-used, light-
weight tweeds in a dark-green herringbone, a soft
white silk shirt and an old school tie – in his case
Wykehamist. At the sight of the tie, and while they

exchanged conventional greetings in the small musty lobby of the apartment, Bond's spirits, already low, sank another degree. He knew the type: backbone of the Civil Service; over-crammed and under-loved at Winchester; a good second in PPE at Oxford; the war, staff jobs he would have done meticulously; perhaps an OBE; Allied Control Commission in Germany where he had been recruited into the I Branch and thence – because he was the ideal staff man and A1 with Security and because he thought he would find life, drama, romance, the things he had never had – into the Secret Service. A sober, careful man had been needed to chaperon Bond on this ugly business. Captain Paul Sender, late of the Welsh Guards, had been the obvious choice. He had bought it. Now, like a good Wykehamist, he concealed his distaste for the job beneath careful, trite conversation as he showed Bond the layout of the apartment and the arrangements that had been made for the executioner's preparedness and, to a modest extent, his comfort.

The flat consisted of a large double bedroom, a bathroom, and a kitchen containing tinned food, milk, butter, eggs, tea, bacon, bread and one bottle of Dimple Haig. The only odd feature in the bedroom was that one of the double beds was angled up against the curtains covering the single broad window and was piled high with three mattresses below the bed-clothes.

Captain Sender said, 'Care to have a look at the

field of fire? Then I can explain what the other side have in mind.'

Bond was tired. He didn't particularly want to go to sleep with the picture of the battlefield on his mind. He said, 'That'd be fine.'

Captain Sender switched off the lights. Chinks from the street light at the intersection showed round the curtains. 'Don't want to draw the curtains,' said Captain Sender. 'Unlikely, but they may be on the look-out for a covering party for 272. If you'd just lie on the bed and get your head under the curtains, I'll brief you about what you'll be looking at. Look to the left.'

It was a sash window and the bottom half was open. The mattress, by design, gave only a little and James Bond found himself more or less in the firing position he had been in on the Century Range, but now staring across broken, thickly weeded bombed ground towards the bright river of the Zimmerstrasse – the border with East Berlin. It looked about a hundred and fifty yards away. Captain Sender's voice from above him and behind the curtain began reciting. It reminded Bond of a spiritualist séance.

'That's bombed ground in front of you. Plenty of cover. A hundred and thirty yards of it up to the frontier. Then the frontier – the street – and then a big stretch of more bombed ground on the enemy side. That's why 272 chose this route. It's one of the few places in the town which is broken land – thick weeds, ruined walls, cellars – on both sides of the frontier. He will sneak through that mess on the other side and make a dash across the Zimmerstrasse for the mess on our side. Trouble is, he'll have thirty yards of brightly lit frontier to sprint across. That'll be the killing ground. Right?'

Bond said, 'Yes.' He said it softly. The scent of the enemy, the need to take care, already had him by the nerves.

'To your left, that big new ten-storey block is the Haus der Ministerien, the chief brain-centre of East Berlin. You can see the lights are still on in most of the windows. Most of those'll stay on all night. These chaps work hard – shifts all round the clock. You probably won't need to worry about the lighted ones. This "Trigger" chap'll almost certainly fire from one of the dark windows. You'll see there's a block of four together on the corner above the intersection. They've stayed dark last night and tonight. They've got the best field of fire. From here, their range varies from three hundred to three hundred and ten yards. I've got all the figures and so on when you want them. You needn't worry about much else. That street stays empty during the night – only the motorized patrols about every half an hour – light armoured car with a couple of motor-cycles as escort. Last night, which I suppose is typical, between six and seven when this thing's going to be done, there were a few people that came and went out of that side door. Civil servant types. Before that nothing out of the ordinary – usual flow of people in and out of a busy government building – except, of all things, a whole damned women's orchestra. Made the hell of a racket in some concert hall they've got in there. Part of the block is the Ministry of Culture. Otherwise nothing – certainly none of the KGB people we know, nor any signs of preparation for a job like this. But there wouldn't be. They're careful chaps, the opposition. Anyway, have a good look. Don't forget it's darker than it will be tomorrow around six. But you can get the general picture.'

Bond got the general picture and it stayed with him long after the other man was asleep and snoring softly with a gentle regular clicking sound – a Wyke-hamist snore, Bond reflected irritably.

Yes, he had got the picture – the picture of a flicker of movement among the shadowy ruins on the other side of the gleaming river of light, a pause, then the wild zigzagging sprint of a man in the full glare of the arcs, the crash of gunfire and either a crumpled, sprawling heap in the middle of the wide street or the noise of his onward dash through the weeds and rubble of the Western Sector – sudden death or a home run. The true gauntlet! How much time would Bond have to spot the Russian sniper in one of those dark windows? And kill him? Five seconds? Ten? When dawn edged the curtains with gun-metal, Bond capitulated to his fretting mind. It had won. He went softly into the bathroom and surveyed the ranks of medicine bottles that a thoughtful Secret Service had provided to keep its executioner in good shape.

He selected the Tuinal, chased down two of the ruby-and-blue depth-charges with a glass of water and went back to bed. Then, pole-axed, he slept.

He awoke at midday. The flat was empty. Bond drew the curtains to let in the grey Prussian day and, standing well back from the window, gazed out at the drabness of Berlin and listened to the tram noises and to the distant screeching of the U-Bahn as it took the big curve into the Zoo station. He gave a quick, reluctant glance at what he had examined the night before, noted that the weeds among the bomb rubble were much the same as the London ones – rose-bay willow-herb, dock and bracken – and then went into the kitchen. There was a note propped against a loaf of bread: 'My friend [a Secret Service euphemism which in this context meant Sender's chief] says it's all right for you to go out. But to be back by 1700 hours. Your gear [double-talk for Bond's rifle] has arrived and the batman will lay it out this pm. P. Sender.'

Bond lit the gas cooker, burned the message with a sneer at his profession, and then brewed himself a vast dish of scrambled eggs and bacon which he heaped on buttered toast and washed down with black coffee into which he had poured a liberal tot of whisky. Then he bathed and shaved, dressed in the drab, anonymous, middle-European clothes he had brought over for the purpose, looked at his disordered bed, decided to hell with it, and went down in the lift and out of the building.

James Bond had always found Berlin a glum, inimical city varnished on the Western side with a brittle veneer of gimcrack polish, rather like the chromium trim on American motor-cars. He walked to the Kurfürstendamm, sat in the Café Marquardt, drank an espresso and moodily watched the obedient queues of pedestrians waiting for the 'Go' sign on the traffic lights while the shiny stream of cars went through their dangerous quadrille at the busy intersection. It was cold outside and the sharp wind from the Russian steppes whipped at the girls' skirts and at the waterproofs of the impatient hurrying men each with the inevitable briefcase tucked under his arm. The infra-red wall heaters in the café glared redly down and gave a spurious glow to the faces of the café-squatters consuming their traditional 'one cup of coffee and ten glasses of water', reading the free newspapers and periodicals in their wooden racks or earnestly bent over business documents. Bond, closing his mind to the evening, debated with himself about ways to spend the afternoon. It finally came down to a choice between a visit to that respectable-looking brownstone house in the Clausewitzstrasse, known to all concierges and taxi-drivers, or a trip to the Wannsee and a strenuous walk in the Grunewald. Virtue triumphed. Bond paid for his coffee, went out into the cold and took a taxi to the Zoo station.

The pretty young trees round the long lake had already been touched by the breath of autumn and there was occasional gold amongst the green. Bond walked hard for two hours along the leafy paths, then chose a restaurant with a glassed-in veranda above the lake and greatly enjoyed a high tea consisting of a double portion of matjes herrings smothered in cream and onion rings, and two 'Molle mit Korn', the Berlin equivalent of a 'boilermaker and his assistant' – schnapps, doubles, washed down with draught Löwenbräu. Then, feeling more encouraged, he took the S-Bahn back into the city.

Outside the apartment house, a nondescript young man was tinkering with the engine of a black Opel Kapitan. He didn't take his head out from under the bonnet when Bond passed close by him and went up to the door and pressed the bell.

Captain Sender was reassuring. It was a 'friend' – a corporal from the transport section of Station WB. He had fixed up some bad engine trouble on the Opel. Each night, from six to seven, he would be ready to produce a series of multiple back-fires when a signal on a walkie-talkie operated by Sender told him to do so. This would give some kind of cover for the noise of Bond's shooting. Otherwise the neighbourhood might alert the police and there would be a lot of untidy explaining to be done. Their hideout was in the American sector and, while their American 'friends' had given Station WB clearance for this operation, the 'friends' were naturally anxious that it should be a clean job and without repercussions.

Bond was suitably impressed by the car gimmick,

as he was by the very workmanlike preparations that had been made for him in the living-room. Here, behind the head of his high bed, giving a perfect firing position, a wood and metal stand had been erected against the broad window-sill and along it lay the Winchester, the tip of its barrel just denting the curtains. The wood and all the metal parts of the rifle and Sniperscope had been painted a dull black and, laid out on the bed like sinister evening clothes, was a black velvet hood stitched to a waist-length shirt of the same material. The hood had wide slits for the eyes and mouth. It reminded Bond of old prints of the Spanish Inquisition, or of the anonymous operators on the guillotine platform during the French Revolution. There was a similar hood on Captain Sender's bed, and on his section of the window-sill there lay a pair of night-glasses and the microphone for the walkie-talkie.

Captain Sender, his face worried and tense with nerves, said there was no news at the Station, no change in the situation as they knew it. Did Bond want anything to eat? Or a cup of tea? Perhaps a tranquillizer – there were several kinds in the bathroom?

Bond stitched a cheerful, relaxed expression on his face and said no thanks, and gave a light-hearted account of his day while an artery near his solar plexus began thumping gently as tension built up inside him like a watch-spring tightening. Finally his small talk petered out and he lay down on his bed with a

German thriller he had bought on his wanderings, while Captain Sender moved fretfully about the flat, looking too often at his watch and chain-smoking Kent filter-tips through (he was a careful man) a Dunhill filter holder.

James Bond's choice of reading matter, prompted by a spectacular jacket of a half-naked girl strapped to a bed, turned out to have been a happy one for the occasion. It was called *Verderbt, Verdammt, Verraten.* The prefix '*ver*' signified that the girl had not only been ruined, damned and betrayed, but that she had suffered these misfortunes most thoroughly. James Bond temporarily lost himself in the tribulations of the heroine, Gräfin Liselotte Mutzenbacher, and it was with irritation that he heard Captain Sender say that it was five thirty and time to take up their positions.

Bond took off his coat and tie, put two sticks of chewing gum in his mouth and donned the hood. The lights were switched off by Captain Sender and Bond lay along the bed, got his eye to the eye-piece of the Sniperscope and gently lifted the bottom edge of the curtain back and over his shoulders.

Now dusk was approaching, but otherwise the scene, a year later to become famous as 'Checkpoint Charlie', was like a well-remembered photograph – the waste-land in front of him, the bright river of the frontier road, the farther waste-land and, on the left, the ugly square block of the Haus der Ministerien with its lit and dark windows. Bond scanned it all slowly, moving the Sniperscope, with the rifle, by means of the precision screws on the wooden base. It was all the same except that now there was a trickle of personnel leaving and entering the Ministry through the door on to the Wilhelmstrasse. Bond looked along at the four dark windows – dark again tonight – that he agreed with Sender were the enemy's firing points. The curtains were drawn back and the sash windows were wide open at the bottom. Bond's 'scope could not penetrate into the rooms, but there was no sign of movement within the four oblong, black, gaping mouths.

Now there was extra traffic in the street below. The women's orchestra came trooping down the pavement towards the entrance – twenty laughing, talking girls carrying their instruments – violin and wind instrument cases, satchels with their scores, and four of them with the drums – a gay, happy little crocodile. Bond was reflecting that some people still seemed to find life fun in the Soviet Sector, when his glasses picked out and stayed on the girl carrying the 'cello. Bond's masticating jaws stopped still and then reflectively went on with their chewing as he twisted the screw to depress the Sniperscope and keep her in its centre.

The girl was taller than the others and her long, straight, fair hair, falling to her shoulders, shone like molten gold under the arcs at the intersection. She was hurrying along in a charming, excited way, carrying the 'cello case as if it were no heavier than a violin. Everything was flying – the skirt of her coat, her feet, her hair. She was vivid with movement and life and, it seemed, with gaiety and happiness as she chattered to the two girls who flanked her and laughed back at what she was saying. As she turned in at the entrance amidst her troupe, the arcs momentarily caught a beautiful, pale profile. And then she was gone and, it seemed to Bond, with her disappearance a stab of grief lanced into his heart. How odd! How very odd! This had not happened to him since he was young. And now this single girl, seen only indistinctly and far away, had caused him to suffer this sharp pang of longing, this thrill of animal magnetism! Morosely, Bond glanced down at the luminous dial of his watch. Five fifty. Only ten minutes to go. No transport arriving at the entrance. None of those anonymous black Zik saloons he had half expected. He closed as much of his mind as he could to the girl and sharpened his wits. Get on, damn you! Get back to your job!

From somewhere inside the Ministry there came the familiar sounds of an orchestra tuning up – the strings tuning their instruments to single notes on the piano, the sharp blare of individual wood-winds – then a pause and then the collective crash of melody as the whole orchestra threw itself competently, so far as Bond could judge, into the opening bars of what even to James Bond was vaguely familiar.

'The Polovtsian Dances from *Prince Igor*,' said Captain Sender succinctly. 'Anyway, six o'clock coming up,' and then, urgently, 'Hey! Right-hand bottom of the four windows! Watch out!'

Bond minutely depressed the Sniperscope. Yes, there was movement inside the black cave. Now, from the interior, a thick black object, a weapon, had slid out. It moved firmly, minutely, swivelling down and sideways so as to cover the stretch of the Zimmerstrasse between the two waste-lands of rubble. Then the unseen operator in the room behind seemed satisfied and the weapon remained still, fixed obviously to a stand such as Bond had beneath his rifle.

'What is it? What sort of gun?' Captain Sender's voice was more breathless than it should have been. Take it easy, dammit! thought Bond. It's me who's supposed to have the nerves.

He strained his eyes, taking in the squat flash eliminator at the muzzle, the telescopic sight and thick downward chunk of magazine. Yes, that would be it! Absolutely for sure – and the best they had!

'Kalashnikov,' he said curtly. 'Sub-machine-gun. Gas-operated. Thirty rounds in 7.62 millimetre. Favourite with the KGB. They're going to do a saturation job after all. Perfect for range. We'll have to get him pretty quick or 272'll end up not just dead but strawberry jam. You keep an eye out for any movement over there in the rubble. I'll have to stay married to that window and the gun. He'll have to show himself to fire. Other chaps are probably spotting behind him – perhaps from all four windows. Much the sort of set-up we expected, but I didn't think they'd use a weapon that's going to make all the racket this one will. Should have known they would. A running man would be hard to get in this light with a single-shot job.'

Bond fiddled minutely with the traversing and elevating screws at his fingertips and got the fine lines of the 'scope exactly intersected, just behind where the butt of the enemy gun merged into the blackness behind. Get the chest – don't bother about the head!

Inside the hood, Bond's face began to sweat and his eye socket was slippery against the rubber of the eye-piece. That didn't matter. It was only his hands, his trigger-finger, that must stay bone dry. As the minutes ticked by, he frequently blinked his eyes to rest them, shifted his limbs to keep them supple, listened to the music to relax his mind.

The minutes slouched on leaden feet. How old would she be? Early twenties – say, twenty-three. With that poise and insouciance, the hint of authority in her long easy stride, she would come of good racy stock – one of the old Prussian families probably, or from similar remnants in Poland or even Russia. Why in hell did she have to choose the 'cello? There was something almost indecent in the idea of that bulbous, ungainly instrument between her splayed thighs. Of course Suggia had managed to look elegant, and so did that girl Amaryllis somebody. But they should invent a way for women to play the damned thing side-saddle.

At his side Captain Sender said, 'Seven o'clock.

Nothing's stirred on the other side. Bit of movement on our side, near a cellar close to the frontier; that'll be our reception committee – two good men from the Station. Better stay with it until they close down. Let me know when they take that gun in.'

'All right.'

It was seven thirty when the KGB sub-machine-gun was gently drawn back into the black interior. One by one the bottom sashes of the four windows were closed. The cold-hearted game was over for the night. 272 was still holed up. Two more nights to go!

Bond softly drew the curtain over his shoulders and across the muzzle of the Winchester. He got up, pulled off his cowl and went into the bathroom and stripped and had a shower. Then he had two large whiskies on the rocks in quick succession, while he waited, his ears pricked, for the now muffled sound of the orchestra to stop. When at eight o'clock it did (with the expert comment from Sender, 'Borodin's *Prince Igor*, Choral Dance Number 17, I think,') he said to Sender, who had been getting off his report in garbled language to the Head of Station, 'Just going to have another look. I've rather taken to that tall blonde with the 'cello.'

'Didn't notice her,' said Sender, uninterested. He went into the kitchen. Tea, guessed Bond. Or perhaps Horlicks. Bond donned his cowl, went back to his firing position and depressed the Sniperscope to the doorway of the Ministry. Yes, there they went, not so gay and laughing now. Tired, perhaps. And now here she came, less lively but still with that beautiful careless stride. Bond watched the blown, golden hair and the fawn raincoat until it had vanished into the indigo dusk up the Wilhelmstrasse. Where did she live? In some miserable, flaked room in the suburbs? Or in one of the privileged apartments in the hideous, lavatory-tiled Stalinallee?

Bond drew himself back. Somewhere, within easy reach, that girl lived. Was she married? Did she have a lover? Anyway to hell with it! She was not for him.

The next day, and the next night-watch, were duplicates, with small variations, of the first. James Bond had two more brief rendezvous, by Sniperscope, with the girl, and the rest was a killing of time and a tightening of the tension that, by the time the third and final day came, was like a fog in the small room.

James Bond crammed the third day with an almost lunatic programme of museums, art galleries, the zoo and a film, hardly perceiving anything he looked at, his mind's eye divided between the girl and those four black squares and the black tube and the unknown man behind it – the man he was now certainly going to kill tonight.

Back in the apartment punctually at five, Bond narrowly averted a row with Captain Sender, because he had poured himself a stiff whisky before putting on the hideous cowl that now stank of his sweat.

Captain Sender had tried to prevent him and, when he failed, had threatened to call up Head of Station and report Bond for breaking training.

'Look, my friend,' said Bond wearily, 'I've got to commit a murder tonight. Not you. Me. So be a good chap and stuff it, would you? You can tell Tanqueray anything you like when it's over. Think I like this job? Having a Double-O number and so on? I'd be quite happy for you to get me sacked from the Double-O Section. Then I could settle down and make a snug nest of papers as an ordinary Staffer. Right?' Bond drank down his whisky, reached for his thriller, now arriving at an appalling climax, and threw himself on the bed.

Captain Sender, icily silent, went off into the kitchen to brew, from the sounds, his inevitable cuppa.

Bond felt the whisky beginning to melt the coiled nerves in his stomach. Now then, Liselotte, how in hell are you going to get out of this fix?

It was exactly six five when Sender, at his post, began talking excitedly. 'Bond, there's something moving way back over there. Now he's stopped – wait, no, he's on the move again, keeping low. There's a bit of broken wall there. He'll be out of sight of the opposition. But thick weeds, yards of them, ahead of him. Christ! He's coming through the weeds. And they're moving. Hope to God they think it's only the wind.

Now he's through and gone to ground. Any reaction?'

'No,' said Bond tensely. 'Keep on telling me. How far to the frontier?'

'He's only got about fifty yards to go.' Captain Sender's voice was harsh with excitement. 'Broken stuff, but some of it's open. Then a solid chunk of wall right up against the pavement. He'll have to get over it. They can't fail to spot him then. Now! Now he's made ten yards, and another ten. Got him clearly then. Blackened his face and hands. Get ready! Any moment now he'll make the last sprint.'

James Bond felt the sweat pouring down his face and neck. He took a chance and quickly wiped his hands down his sides and then got them back to the rifle, his finger inside the guard, just lying along the curved trigger. 'There's something moving in the room behind the gun. They must have spotted him. Get that Opel working.'

Bond heard the code word go into the microphone, heard the Opel in the street below start up, felt his pulse quicken as the engine leaped into life and a series of ear-splitting cracks came from the exhaust.

The movement in the black cave was now definite. A black arm with a black glove had reached out and under the stock.

'Now!' ejaculated Captain Sender. 'Now! He's run for the wall! He's up it! Just going to jump!'

And then, in the Sniperscope, Bond saw the head of 'Trigger' – the purity of the profile, the golden bell

of hair – all laid out along the stock of the Kalashnikov! She was dead, a sitting duck! Bond's fingers
flashed down to the screws, inched them round and,
as yellow flame fluttered at the snout of the sub-
machine-gun, squeezed the trigger.

The bullet, dead on at three hundred and ten yards,
must have hit where the stock ended up the barrel,
might have got her in the left hand, but the effect
was to tear the gun off its mountings, smash it
against the side of the window-frame and then hurl it
out of the window. It turned several times on its way
down and crashed into the middle of the street.

'He's over!' shouted Captain Sender. 'He's over!
He's done it! My God, he's done it!'

'Get down!' said Bond sharply, and threw himself
sideways off the bed as the big eye of a searchlight in
one of the black windows blazed on, swerving up the
street towards their block and their room. Then gunfire crashed and the bullets howled into their window,
ripping the curtains, smashing the woodwork, thud-
ding into the walls.

Behind the roar and zing of the bullets, Bond heard
the Opel race off down the street and, behind that
again, the fragmentary whisper of the orchestra. The
combination of the two background noises clicked.
Of course! The orchestra had probably raised an
infernal din throughout the Haus der Ministerien,
having been used, like the back-firing Opel on this
side, to provide some cover for a sharp burst of
fire, on their side by 'Trigger'. Had she carried

her weapon to and fro every day in that 'cello case? Was the whole orchestra composed of KGB women? Had the other instrument cases contained only equipment – the big drum perhaps the search-light – while the real instruments were available in the concert hall? Too elaborate? Too fantastic? Prob-ably. But there had been no doubt about the girl. In the Sniperscope, Bond had even been able to see one wide, heavily lashed, aiming eye. Had he hurt her? Almost certainly her left arm. There would be no chance of seeing her, seeing how she was, if she left with the orchestra. Now he would never see her again. Their window would be a death trap. To underline the fact, a stray bullet smashed into the mechanism of the Winchester, already overturned and damaged, and hot lead splashed down on Bond's hand, burning the skin. On Bond's emphatic oath, abruptly the firing stopped and silence sang in the room.

Captain Sender emerged from beside his bed, brushing glass out of his hair. They crunched across the floor and through the splintered door into the kitchen. Here, because it faced away from the street, it was safe to switch on the light.

'Any damage?' asked Bond.

'No. You all right?' Captain Sender's pale eyes were bright with the fever that comes in battle. They also, Bond noticed, held a sharp glint of accusation.

'Yes. Just get an Elastoplast for my hand. Caught a splash from one of the bullets.' Bond went into the bathroom. When he came out, Captain Sender was sitting by the walkie-talkie he had fetched from the sitting-room. He was speaking into it. Now he said into the microphone, 'That's all for now. Fine about 272. Hurry the armoured car, if you would. Be glad to get out of here, and 007 will need to write his version of what happened. Okay? Then OVER and OUT.'

Captain Sender turned to Bond. Half accusing, half embarrassed, he said, 'Afraid Head of Station needs your reasons in writing for not getting that chap. I had to tell him I'd seen you alter your aim at the last second. Gave "Trigger" time to get off a burst. Damned lucky for 272 he'd just begun his sprint. Blew chunks off the wall behind him. What was it all about?'

James Bond knew he could lie, knew he could fake a dozen reasons why. Instead he took a deep pull at the strong whisky he had poured for himself, put the glass down and looked Captain Sender straight in the eye.

' "Trigger" was a woman.'

'So what? KGB have got plenty of women agents – and women gunners. I'm not in the least surprised. The Russian women's team always does well in the World Championships. Last meeting, in Moscow, they came first, second and third against seven countries. I can even remember two of their names – Donskaya and Lomova, terrific shots. She may even have been one of them. What did she look like? Records'll probably be able to turn her up.'

'She was a blonde. She was the girl who carried the 'cello in that orchestra. Probably had her gun in the 'cello case. The orchestra was to cover up the shooting.'

'Oh!' said Captain Sender slowly, 'I see. The girl you were keen on?'

'That's right.'

'Well, I'm sorry, but I'll have to put that in my report too. You had clear orders to exterminate "Trigger".'

There came the sound of a car approaching. It pulled up somewhere below. The bell rang twice. Sender said, 'Well, let's get going. They've sent an armoured car to get us out of here.' He paused. His eyes flicked over Bond's shoulder, avoiding Bond's eyes. 'Sorry about the report. Got to do my duty, y'know. You should have killed that sniper whoever it was.'

Bond got up. He suddenly didn't want to leave the stinking little smashed-up flat, leave the place from which, for three days, he had had this long-range, one-sided romance with an unknown girl – an unknown enemy agent with much the same job in her outfit as he had in his. Poor little bitch! She would be in worse trouble now than he was! She'd certainly be court-martialled for muffing this job. Probably be kicked out of the KGB. He shrugged. At least they'd stop short of killing her – as he himself had done.

James Bond said wearily, 'Okay. With any luck it'll cost me my Double-O number. But tell Head of

Station not to worry. That girl won't do any more sniping. Probably lost her left hand. Certainly broke her nerve for that kind of work. Scared the living daylights out of her. In my book, that was enough. Let's go.'

Ian Fleming
Diamonds Are Forever 45p

'Combines the tough-tender glamour of the
sado-masochistic, Casanova-esque private eye with the
connoisseurship of a member of White's, laces this already
heady mixture with a shot of the Buchanish Imperialistic
spirit, and adds a tiny pinch of ground Ashenden'
OBSERVER

Moonraker 35p

'James Bond's companion is as smashing a lovely as any
predecessor in the role, the villain as sulphurously infernal,
the declaration of war as dramatic' SCOTSMAN

Casino Royale 60p

'The best gambling scene one can recall, and the most
revolting of torture scenes' BIRMINGHAM POST

Also available

The Man with the Golden Gun	60p
Live and Let Die	40p
On Her Majesty's Secret Service	45p
You Only Live Twice	45p
From Russia with Love	60p
Thunderball	60p
Goldfinger	60p
Dr No	60p
For Your Eyes Only	60p

Peter O'Donnell

Author of the thrilling novels about Modesty Blaise –
'One of the great desperadoes . . . and the books in which
the adventures of herself, Willie Garvin, the manservant
Weng, and the Secret Service chief Tarrant appear are
literate, pacey, exciting and captivating' SPECTATOR

Modesty Blaise 60p

'Comparisons of Modesty with James Bond are irresistible.
The similarities are marked – the restless changing scenes,
the ingenuity of both sides, the violence, the surging
confidence in telling' EVENING STANDARD

Sabre-Tooth 60p

'I don't recommend anyone to start on it, because the fact
is that once you have begun it's very hard to put down'
DAILY TELEGRAPH

I, Lucifer 50p

'Modesty never had more lethal adversaries: Lucifer,
whose world is fantasy; Seff, who gives unspeakable puppet
shows, and Jack Wise, the executioner. Readably different'
SHEFFIELD MORNING TELEGRAPH

A Taste for Death 50p

'No one could find fault with Peter O'Donnell for
excitement, detail and ingenuity' OXFORD MAIL

The Impossible Virgin 60p

'The story has everything – violence, sex, torture,
man-to-man combat, spy-stuff, medicine . . . Great fun!'
NEW YORK TIMES

Selected bestsellers

☐ **Jaws** Peter Benchley 70p
☐ **Let Sleeping Vets Lie** James Herriot 60p
☐ **If Only They Could Talk** James Herriot 60p
☐ **It Shouldn't Happen to a Vet** James Herriot 60p
☐ **Vet in Harness** James Herriot 60p
☐ **Tinker Tailor Soldier Spy** John le Carré 60p
☐ **Alive: The Story of the Andes Survivors** (illus)
   Piers Paul Read 75p
☐ **Gone with the Wind** Margaret Mitchell £1.50
☐ **Mandingo** Kyle Onstott 75p
☐ **Shout at the Devil** Wilbur Smith 70p
☐ **Cashelmara** Susan Howatch £1.25
☐ **Hotel** Arthur Hailey 80p
☐ **The Tower** Richard Martin Stern 70p
   (filmed as *The Towering Inferno*)
☐ **Bonecrack** Dick Francis 60p
☐ **Jonathan Livingston Seagull** Richard Bach 80p
☐ **The Fifth Estate** Robin Moore 75p
☐ **Royal Flash** George MacDonald Fraser 60p
☐ **The Nonesuch** Georgette Heyer 60p
☐ **Murder Most Royal** Jean Plaidy 80p
☐ **The Grapes of Wrath** John Steinbeck 95p

All these books are available at your bookshop or newsagent;
or can be obtained direct from the publisher
Just tick the titles you want and fill in the form below
Prices quoted are applicable in UK

Pan Books, Cavaye Place, London SW10 9PG
Send purchase price plus 15p for the first book and 5p for each
additional book, to allow for postage and packing

Name (block letters)_____

Address_____

_____

While every effort is made to keep prices low, it is sometimes
necessary to increase prices at short notice. Pan Books reserve the
right to show on covers new retail prices which may differ from
those advertised in the text or elsewhere